THE BULL RIDER'S REDEMPTION

—

Heidi Hormel

HARLEQUIN® WESTERN ROMANCE®

Recycling programs
for this product may
not exist in your area.

ISBN-13: 978-0-373-75729-9

The Bull Rider's Redemption

Printed in U.S.A.

www.Harlequin.com

"Clover Van Camp doesn't have a boyfriend!" Danny teased.

Clover shook her head. "Nope, I've been focusing on work. What about you?"

"Nah. Between my business and being mayor, I just don't have the time."

"Didn't you say you could *always* make time for the ladies?"

"I said that in an interview when I was twenty-one and just won a buckle!" Danny laughed. "So...you kept up with me?"

She may have followed his career...a little. She blushed. "I followed everyone I knew from bull riding."

"Good recovery." He laughed again, his blue eyes bright with humor. "Well, I'd better get going."

"It was good to visit." She smiled.

"Same here." He didn't move, his gaze on her face.

Her breath quickened just a little. Danny grinned as he put out his hand for a shake. As she grasped his strong hand she felt that old flush of heat and desire working its way through her. How could that be, more than ten years after *that* summer?

She tugged him toward her...and Danny didn't hesitate.

Dear Reader,

Danny Leigh was nearly shouting at me to tell his story. The trouble was that where his story started is not where it ended up. He and his first love, a Texas cowgirl with New York blue-blood roots, taught me that changing horses midstream isn't easy, but it makes the destination that much sweeter. Of course, I got Danny back, torturing him just a little in this Angel Crossing, Arizona, book. Bwa-ha-ha.

At the heart of this reunion romance are two people just trying to do the best they can: Mayor Danny working to improve his town by remaining true to its roots and Clover Van Camp planning to transform the community into a Wild West resort with jobs and prosperity for one and all. Of course, the residents of Angel Crossing aren't going to let this battle play out without putting in their two cents every chance they get.

I have so many more stories to tell about Angel Crossing and I can't wait to do that. When I look back on how this all started with *The Surgeon and the Cowgirl*, I do wonder what the inspiration fairies were drinking.

If you want to know more about my inspirations and musings or drop me a note, check out my website and blog at heidihormel.net, where you also can sign up for my newsletter; or connect with me at Facebook.com/AuthorHeidiHormel; on Twitter @HeidiHormel; or Pinterest.com/hhormel.

Yee-Haw,

Heidi Hormel

With stints as an innkeeper and radio talk show host, **Heidi Hormel** settled into her true calling as a writer by spending years as a reporter (covering the story of the rampaging elephants Debbie and Tina) and as a PR flunky (staying calm in the face of Cookiegate). Now she is happiest penning romances with a wink and a wiggle.

A small-town girl from the Snack Food Capital of the World, Heidi has trotted over a good portion of the globe, from Tombstone in Arizona to Loch Ness in Scotland to the depths of Death Valley. She draws on all of these experiences for her books, but especially her annual visits to the Grand Canyon state for her Angel Crossing, Arizona, series.

Heidi is on the web at heidihormel.net, as well as socially out there at Facebook.com/authorheidihormel, Twitter.com/heidihormel and Pinterest.com/hhormel.

Books by Heidi Hormel

Harlequin American Romance

The Surgeon and the Cowgirl
The Convenient Cowboy
The Accidental Cowboy
The Kentucky Cowboy's Baby

Visit the Author Profile page
at Harlequin.com for more titles.

To my hometown for giving me
too much inspiration—I'll never have
the time to write all these books!

Chapter One

Just like riding a bike, my aunt Fanny. The weighted edge of Clover Van Camp's sequined, tailored gown and her three-inch stilettos were parts of a life she'd left years ago, when she'd gone to college and finally convinced her mother that statistics class would get her further in the fashion industry than pageants. This was a one-night only return to the stage as a beauty queen. Her mother had promised.

Clover handed the award to the man in the cowboy hat and Western tuxedo with buttons straining over his middle. She stood behind him as he spoke about his philanthropy to the crowded Phoenix ballroom. Her smile was pleasant, masking a desperate desire to move her pinned and sprayed head of "naturally tousled" red hair. *La-di-da and fiddly dee*, she said to herself, the joys of being a vice president of events for her mother's fashion house. The clapping prompted her to step forward to direct the winner to the spot for his photo with the Junior League's president. As she maneuvered him into position, his hand squeezed her sequined, Spanxed butt.

"What the hell?" she yelped, pushing him and knocking him off balance and into the Junior League president. Clover watched as the pinwheeling man and woman sprawled onto the wooden floor, as Grabby Hands' white Stetson rolled off the stage. Crap. What was it with her and cowboys, gowns and trophies? That was exactly how she'd "fallen" for tall, blond, blue-eyed Danny Leigh years ago. She'd handed him the Junior Championship Bull Rider trophy and, in trying to get herself close to him for the picture, she'd stepped on his cowboy boot with the thin heel of her stiletto, skewering his foot and sending him into a jig that had them both tumbling from the platform.

Now in the Phoenix ballroom more than a decade later, this audience laughed politely, and Clover went on as if nothing had happened. She'd learned how to tape her breasts for the best cleavage and how to smile through anything on the pageant circuit. Good thing, too. She figured tonight's spectacular cleavage (thanks to her taping skills) might make the cowboy forget she'd knocked him to the ground.

Two hours later and on the way to the airport for a red-eye flight back to Austin, Texas, Clover finally read the text from her mother: WTH. U punched award winner?

No punch. Accident. Will explain at office.

By then Clover would have a better, and more PR-friendly, explanation than that Grabby Hands should have kept his mitts off her. She'd already salvaged the situation to the best advantage for her mother's brand—Cowgirl's Blues. In two days, everyone would be talking about the new jeans that lifted butts and flattened tummies, not Clover's stumble. Oh, the glamour of working in the fashion industry.

Was this what she'd pictured when she'd smiled for the camera with her new MBA diploma in hand? She was no closer to a position of real responsibility than a polecat with a ten-foot pole. Of anyone, her mother should be able to understand Clover's ambition to be more than a clothes hanger with breasts. Clover wanted to be the kind of businesswoman her mother was, one who made her mark on an industry.

Why did she have to explain anything to her mother? Clover shouldn't have been forced into the gown and into a position that should have been filled by an intern. The jet flew through the darkened sky and Clover made a decision she'd been working up to since her father had tempted her with a dream job: CFO of Van Camp Worldwide. She'd be second only to her father in power. But it wasn't just the power that mattered—it was also the fact that the position as chief financial officer would allow her to finally use her crazy fast and nearly supernatural ability to look at numbers and see where the problems were. She was done with fashion and more than done trying to please her mother and her Texas-sized ego. Why had she ever imagined that her mother would loosen her grasp on the reins of Cowgirl's Blues?

CLOVER SHOVED HER foot hard into the stiff boots she hadn't worn since…well, since that summer, the one where she'd met Danny Leigh, lost her virginity and had her heart broken all in the space of a few weeks. Ahh, youth was wasted on youth. She grinned until she remembered her mission. She'd accepted her father's challenge, after two weeks' notice to her mother, who told her to leave immediately and not let the door hit her on the way out. Clover's job over the next few months for her father was to prove her worth by convincing property owners and the town council that creating a resort out of Angel Crossing was the best way to save the Arizona town.

She checked over the packed luggage—jeans, cowgirl shirts and plain white undergarments. She needed to dress her part from her skin to her hat. Sure, the town would know her and her purpose. After all, Danny was the mayor now. She wondered if her father had sent her here because he remembered her relationship with the junior champion bull rider. Maybe. Her genius with numbers was matched by her father's photographic memory.

Clover didn't care. She was on her way, and if she needed to use an old relationship to get what she wanted? So be it.

"HEY, BIDDER, BIDDER." The auctioneer started his patter as the sun beat down on Danny's cowboy hat. He was waiting for someone to start the bidding. Then when it looked like the property was ready to sell, he'd jump in. The buildings at the very end of Miner's Gulch, Angel Crossing's main thoroughfare, were perfect for his plans because they were cheap, on large lots.

The crowd was sparse. Good. Probably meant the price would be even lower than he'd hoped. Finally the auctioneer accepted a bid. Danny held his number at his side. He didn't want to jump into the bidding too early. Someone behind him and to the left upped the price by $2,000. The auctioneer looked pained.

"Come on, folks," he said. "These properties are worth a whole lot more than that."

That little push got another person to up the price. Then Danny nearly bid when the auctioneer looked like he was going to call everything done.

"You're making me work for my money, aren't you? I see John back there. Are you bidding?" Silence. Danny saw the auctioneer lifting the gavel to start the count down.

Danny held up his number and nodded. He was sure he'd be the winning bidder now... Then a feminine voice said, "$155,000."

That put the properties near the top of his price range. He and the all-male crowd looked around for the woman in their midst. Though he was tall, all he saw were hats. The high desert where his town sat might not get boiling temperatures—except in the dead of summer—but the sun was just as fierce as anywhere else in the Grand Canyon State.

"Mayor?" the auctioneer asked. Danny nodded and gestured that he'd match the bid and add $1,000. The bidder's voice sounded familiar but wasn't an Angelite.

"It's back to you, Mayor. The little lady does seem determined."

Danny nodded and added $2,000 to her bid of $166,000. He'd already gone beyond what he had to spend. She must have nodded because the auctioneer pointed at Danny again. Damn. If he begged friends and family he might be able to cover the check. He did more calculations in his head. Could he still come out with a little bit of profit after converting the properties? He had to shake his head no. Converting the old warehouses into homes might put money in his pocket in the long term and make Angel Crossing a better place, but he'd be in the red on the project for longer than he could afford. Maybe if he was still bringing in the big purses from his bull rides. But not now.

"Sold," the auctioneer said. "To the lady in the pink hat." Now Danny saw her. About the same height as the men around her, although she'd still be shorter than him. He had to know who'd just bought a chunk of his town. He quickly moved toward her as she walked to the legal eagles ready to sign over the properties as is.

"Pardon, ma'am," Danny said, raising his voice a little to catch her attention. She turned and he stopped. Hells no. "Clover?"

She smiled, her perpetually red lips looking as lush and kissable as they had been during that rodeo summer. The one where he'd won his buckle, lassoed a beauty queen and lost his virginity.

"Hello, Danny," she said, a light drawl in her voice. "I heard you were mayor here. Congratulations." She smiled again. Not the real one he'd come to love, but the staged one that stretched her lips, lifting her cheeks but never reaching her bluebonnet eyes.

"Why?" he asked, not exactly sure what he meant.

"Good investment." She turned back to the paperwork.

Danny wouldn't be dismissed this time. He'd let her take the lead when they'd been teens because she was older than him by two years. He'd seen her as a woman of the world. Not now. Not all of these years later. He wasn't a horny sixteen-year-old with more hormones than brains.

"What exactly do you plan to do with the properties?"

She continued to sign where the official from the county tax sale office pointed but didn't answer.

"I'm mayor and chair of the revitalization committee," he added. True, though the "revitalization committee" was just him. He wanted Angel Crossing to thrive and he had plans that built on some of the changes that were already taking place. He didn't want any of that to be ruined.

Clover nodded but didn't turn. He was starting to get annoyed. He didn't expect her to fall all over herself for an old boyfriend or even because he was mayor. He did expect her to be courteous enough to answer his very legitimate questions. He wasn't moving until she did. Folding his arms over his chest, he stared at her…hat—not her jean-clad rear and long legs. It didn't look like she starved herself anymore. Her mother had been big on her daughter becoming a model for her clothing line, so Clover had watched every morsel that passed her lips. He remembered her almost drooling while he'd eaten a greasy, powdered-sugar-covered funnel cake. It had taken the enjoyment out of eating it.

Slowly, deliberately, he thought, she put down the pen and took the papers before turning to him. Her expression was pleasant even without her wide smile. "What did you need, Danny?"

"I don't *need* anything. I would like to know your plans for the properties, strictly as an official of the town."

"I don't think so." She looked him in the eye, nearly

his height in her impractical pink cowgirl boots, matched to her cowgirl shirt—probably one of her mother's designs. She looked the same, yet different. A woman grown into and comfortable with her blue-blood nose and creamy Southern-belle skin.

"There must be some reason you won't share your plans."

"It's business, Danny. That's all. You were bidding against me. You must have your own plans." There was a question in there somewhere.

"I'm mayor. Of course I have plans. But you work for a clothing designer, don't you?"

"I understood you only became mayor because you lost a card game."

That damned story. It had gotten picked up by a bunch of papers and repeated on a ton of websites. "Not exactly."

She smiled politely. Waiting.

"The vote for mayor was a tie and we drew cards to decide the winner." He didn't need to tell her that he'd been a write-in candidate as a joke. He could have turned it down, but by then he'd decided to step away from bull riding while he was at the top of the profession—he'd just won his champion buckle. That was what he'd told the reporters. It was true enough. He'd had his place in Angel Crossing and the town seemed as good as any to put down roots after years on the road. Anyway, who wouldn't want to be mayor, he'd thought at the time, imagining all kinds of cool things he could do.

"Drawing cards. That's very Wild West, isn't it?"

"I guess. But I'm still mayor."

"Well, it was nice to see you, Danny." She turned from him before he could say anything else. Damn. What was he going to do now? He watched Clover walk away. A beautiful sight, as it always had been. Tall, curvier than she'd been at eighteen and proud. He knew she worked for her mother. A friend of a rodeo friend had told him that years ago, thinking he'd be interested. He hadn't been.

Now, though, what she was up to was important to Angel Crossing. He wasn't the big dumb cowboy who was led around by his gonads anymore. He was a responsible adult who had a town to look after.

CLOVER KEPT HER head high and her steps confident as she walked away from Danny. She could feel his eyes on her. She refused to acknowledge that she knew he was watching. She definitely didn't want him to know that the corner of her heart still ruled by her teenage self liked his denim-blue gaze on her.

Clover disciplined her thoughts by going over the numbers and how these properties fit in with the ones that Van Camp Worldwide already owned. The buildings were slated for demolition, despite their sturdy brick walls. Most places in Angel Crossing were made of wood or adobe, but not these. What had Danny planned for them? Didn't matter. They were hers... well, VCW's.

She walked to the small, fully furnished house she'd rented—simpler than staying at the hotel nearly half an hour away or in Tucson. There used to be an old grand dame of a hotel in Angel Crossing, but it had closed years ago and sat empty, beginning to sag and rot. The town had little future on its current path. It would end up like the other Arizona ghost towns, a place on the map that tourists visited hoping to see spirits of the Wild West.

Next on her to-do list was finding the owners of six other key properties. She had done what she could from New York, but she needed to go to the courthouse in Tucson to start pulling records. She got in her rental car and fired up the GPS, telling her phone to call her brother, Knox, so she could speak with him about the purchase and any other issues he might know about, having worked for their father for years.

It took extra rings for her brother to answer, but he was willing to talk.

"Make sure the attorneys go through the deeds and the town's regulations with a fine-tooth comb," Knox said around a yawn. It was early, early in Hong Kong. "They'll assume they're a bunch of yahoos and blow off a full review."

"I'm on my way to Tucson to check on the ownership of the other properties. I should be able to straighten that out by the end of the day. I think the purchases will be completed faster than we'd calculated. Good thing because this town is definitely on a downward slide."

"What about the mayor?" Knox asked. She could picture her dark-haired brother squinting at his phone because he'd left his glasses somewhere.

There was more to the question than what sat on the surface.

"You mean, what's it like catching up with an old

boyfriend? We were kids. He's just a retired bull rider and accidental mayor of a dying town."

"You might be interested to know that he's been buying properties along the main street—Miner's Gulch."

"That explains why he was bidding against us today."

"Interesting. Do you think he's a front man for another company?"

Clover was getting used to the suspicion and worry that ran through VCW. "I doubt it. I don't see Danny Leigh allowing himself to be used that way, but I'll have New York check into it if you think it's important." Maybe she should meet with Danny to figure out why he'd wanted the properties. All business. Clover was no longer the beauty-queen cowgirl looking for her one and only cowboy. She had plans, including turning Angel Crossing into Rico Pueblo. With that accomplished, her father would make her CFO. It might feel good, too, knowing that she'd fix something Knox had messed up—for the first time in their lives, maybe.

"If you have any other questions, just give me a call," Knox said. Why was he being so nice? "It's great having you with the company."

"Thanks," Clover said before she hung up. She didn't really believe Knox wished her well. They had always been in competition, especially for their parents' attention. He'd agreed to help her now, even though their father had sent him to Hong Kong. She knew there was more to his banishment to the China office than he was letting on.

She shook her head, wondering if siblings ever got past being ten-year-olds with each other.

Outdoing Knox wasn't childish, though. It would get her the job she'd trained for at the Wharton business school and really start her life as an adult. No more picking out tablecloth colors or deciding whether roses or lilies were better in the centerpieces, as she'd done for Cowgirl's Blues. She would be reshaping a town and leading VCW into an entirely new business venture. First, though, she needed to find the owners of the next properties on her list, then make offers. That would provide VCW with enough land to begin the process of rezoning.

CLOVER TURNED ONTO Miner's Gulch—the name of the street would need to be changed. Picturesque for a ghost town, but not so much for a fun, yet sophisticated village and resort that would be Rico Pueblo. She reached for her phone on the passenger seat to record a reminder about the street name. Where was it? She turned to look and saw that it had slid out of reach. She glanced back to the road. "Oh, no!" she said, seeing a dog cowering in her path. She slammed on her brakes and swerved just as the dog unfroze and ran toward her turning car. The thud of car into dog made Clover wince and cry out.

She couldn't see the animal. Her heart beat in her ears. She put the vehicle in Park, her hands shaking as she turned off the engine and hurried out of the car. She didn't want to look. She didn't want to see the animal's mangled body. But it might be alive. She walked toward the side that would have hit the dog. No body, but there were drops of blood. She'd definitely hit the dog. She left the car and followed the trail of red dots toward an alley. Should she call someone for help? Her first thought was Danny. No. She'd deal with whatever she found when she reached the end of the blood trail.

Chapter Two

A howl lifted the hairs on the back of Danny's neck. Not a coyote, though they did creep into town. Definitely a dog, and one in distress. Danny stopped for a moment, listening to figure out where it was. His own hound had died just after he'd stopped riding bulls. He hadn't been able to make himself adopt another.

He moved as a whine echoed off the wooden facades of the buildings. The animal was definitely in pain. He stopped again, squinting down the sidewalk for the dog or someone looking for it. Whimpering drifted to him from his left, down a short alley that led to a parking lot. He hurried as the whimper scaled back up to a howl.

"Doggie," a female voice said as he rushed down the narrow passage and toward the lot. He scanned the empty area until he noticed a woman standing near a Dumpster. The whimper changed to a growl. Didn't she know what that meant? That was more than a warning.

"Hey," he yelled. She whipped around as a dirty dog darted away despite a heavy limp.

"Darn it," Clover said because, of course, it had to be Clover. "I finally had him cornered."

"You're lucky you didn't get bitten."

"I have on gloves and I have a coat to cover him," she said, moving past Danny. "He won't have gone far. Could you call the police for help?"

"I'll help." They walked toward a narrow space between the buildings, too small for a vehicle but large enough for a dog or a person.

Clover pulled a tiny light from her huge purse. She shone it into the darkness. The dog's eyes glowed, its teeth bared as he growled long and low.

Danny put his hand on Clover's arm. "Wait. I don't want either of us to get bitten. Give me the coat. You go around to the other end to keep him from getting away. But don't go near him."

"This is all my fault. He came out of nowhere. I couldn't stop—"

He didn't want to hear her confession now. "Have you ever had a dog?" She didn't answer. "I didn't think so. I grew up around dogs and cattle and every other ornery animal there is. We have to be careful."

She handed him her coat and jogged around the building. He waited for her to appear at the other end of the narrow passageway. The dog was whimpering again in a way that made Danny want to rush to him. Finally, he saw Clover and the dog did, too. It turned to her, and Danny moved slowly forward with the coat in front of him. By the time the dog looked his way, Danny was close enough to drop the Pendleton-patterned jacket over him. Clover hurried from her end of the lane. In the dimness, she whispered over the dog's low growls and whimpers, "What do we do now?"

"Wait until he calms down. Then we're going to use the strap on your purse to lead him out of here."

"This is an Alexander McQueen," Clover said.

"Do you want to save this dog?"

She didn't reply, instead taking the strap off her purse, and two minutes later he lifted the brightly colored coat off the dog enough to reveal a dirty collar—thank God. He hadn't been sure how else he would have gotten the lead on the animal. He clicked on the "leash" and the dog froze. Then Danny lifted the coat at the same time he pulled up on the lead to keep control of its head. After a few feeble attempts to snap, the fight went out of the creature. Its medium-length matted fur was mostly white with brownish-red patches and ears that drooped. Danny could see the gleam of blood on its flank.

There wasn't a vet in town and the nearest was an hour away. But he knew who could help. Angel Crossing's physician's assistant Pepper Bourne treated humans; she could care for dogs, too. He hoped. "Clover, can you get to your phone?"

"Are you going to call the dog catcher?" she accused.

"I want you to phone Angel Crossing Medical Clinic and speak with Pepper Bourne. I bet she can fix him up."

"Oh." Clover sounded both confused and a little sorry. He gently led the limping and whimpering dog from the lane. He only half listened to Clover's side of the phone conversation.

"Pepper says she can't work on him at the clinic. Can you take him out to the ranch?"

"Tell her we'll be there in twenty minutes."

"Thank you," Clover said. She stepped forward. He moved his head a fraction of an inch, from habit, from want, and the peck she'd been ready to land on his cheek found its home on his lips. Like biting into the ripest peach, the taste of her exploded in his mouth. He pulled her close with his free arm. She didn't protest. Her mouth opened under his and the peaches became spicy with need. This was not the kiss of fumbling, horny teens. This had nothing to do with their past at all. This was its own connection. One that Danny hadn't known before. He deepened the kiss, explored her mouth and her amazing curves. None of it was enough because of this suddenly huge feeling between them.

The dog yanked on its leash and he stepped away. The ache and the need were not what he wanted. He hadn't kissed her for that. He had kissed her because—

"Let's go," he said, knowing his voice growled like the dog's. He didn't care. He was only helping her now because he couldn't let this dog suffer.

"You're LUCKY I keep a kit here at the house," Pepper said as she stitched. At least Clover assumed the other woman with a honey-colored ponytail was stitching, since Clover had stopped watching.

"We need a vet closer than Tucson," Danny commented.

"I know. It costs us a fortune when we bring someone here for Faye's walking yarn balls, aka my mother's alpacas and llamas," she said to Clover. "Hang on. This might be a problem."

"What?" Danny asked anxiously. She remembered the dog he'd had when they'd first met. It'd had only one eye.

"She's pregnant."

"She? Puppies?" Danny sounded both stunned and aggrieved. "Who would dump her?"

Clover's stomach lurched. She'd hit a pregnant dog? Jeez. If there was ever a reason to go to hell, that had to be it. "Do you think they'll be okay?"

"I can feel them moving, so I guess they're good. Since I can feel them, I would also say that she's fairly far along. You'll have to take her to the vet to know for certain. The wound wasn't as bad as it looked. I'd keep her quiet for the next couple of days and come back in a week for me to take the stitches out, if you can't get to the vet or her owner doesn't come forward. Definitely keep a bandage on it in the meantime."

If Clover hadn't felt so bad for the dog, she would have laughed at Danny's stunned face. "Thanks. What do we owe you?" she asked.

"No charge," Pepper said. "Faye wouldn't let me. This is Angel Crossing."

Clover didn't know what that comment meant. Danny lifted the dog carefully and carried it…her to the truck. Puppies. This had gotten complicated quick.

"What was the name of your dog?" Clover asked when they were on the road with the dog's head on Danny's lap, where she was snoring softly. The rest of her limp body draped across the old-fashioned bench seat of his pickup and half onto Clover's lap.

"Which one?"

"The one you had when we met. He only had one eye."

"That was Jack because of the eye."

"I don't get it," she said after a moment of trying to make the connection.

"Like the card. The one-eyed Jack."

A laugh leaked out. "You never told me that."

"We weren't big on talking."

She couldn't deny that. Most of their conversations had been about how to fool around and make sure no one found out. What a summer that had been. So exciting and happy and sad and scary, especially looking back and knowing that she'd nearly ditched college to be with Danny. And the kiss they'd just shared? The one neither of them seemed willing to acknowledge now. The dog whimpered, and she reached out to soothe her.

Danny spoke again. "We had a good time."

She smiled because that was what she'd been more or less thinking. They'd been like that, finishing each other's sentences, or he'd call her just as she got her phone out to call him. "It was a long time ago, and we were very young."

"Not you. You were eighteen. A woman of experience."

"That just meant I'd been somewhere other than a ranch or a rodeo. You know I was a—" She stopped herself because what she would say next sounded so silly and juvenile. They'd both been virgins when they'd finally been able to sneak off for a few hours one night. They'd done the deed. She'd refused to admit it to him or anyone else at the time, but it had been a huge disappointment.

"Two virgins do not a good night make," he said. "It's not polite to talk about other ladies, but I'll just say I've learned a bit since then."

"This is where I should say 'me, too,' but ladies definitely don't say that sort of thing, as my grandmother Van Camp would remind me. My Texas grandmother… She'd say, 'Thank God you're only a heifer once.'" They both laughed. The dog yipped, and Clover rubbed her fur. The poor animal.

"What are we going to do with her?" he asked as he turned onto the main road to town. "I'll check for an owner, but I'm sure she was abandoned."

"I'm not staying here long and my New York condo forbids pets, even goldfish," she said.

"I've got a no-pets sort of place, too."

"You don't have a dog? You said that a cowboy isn't a cowboy without a dog."

"I was sixteen."

Teenagers were allowed to make pronouncements like that before they learned how the world really worked.

"You're the mayor. Can't you make a rule to allow you to keep the dog at your place?"

He laughed. "I wish it worked that way. Maybe Chief Rudy knows someone. The police know everyone."

"You've really settled in here, haven't you? I assumed you wouldn't retire until you couldn't walk anymore."

"Not much choice when I became mayor."

"How could you get written in for mayor? You weren't actually living here if you were still competing."

"Since Gene was here. Do you remember him? He kept AJ and me in line and helped us figure out the bulls. Anyway, Gene had a ranch here, so I decided this would be as good a place as any to call home. I gave this as my address. The next thing I know, I'm mayor. It all happened kind of quick." He didn't look at her, but she saw that he had his signature half smile.

The one that had made her heart flutter—hers and every other girl in the arena.

"That still doesn't explain how you wound up retired."

"A story for another time," he said. "What are we going to do with mama dog?"

Clover had grown up a lot since that summer. Danny's charm—his kisses, too—didn't make her brain short-circuit anymore. "She can't come with me. You have to know someone who will look after her. I'd be willing to pay."

His smile disappeared. "Money doesn't solve everything, you know. That's not how things work here in Angel Crossing. Don't worry about Mama. I'll figure something out."

How could she have forgotten his pride? Prickly and strong. Maybe that was why he fit so well in Arizona. He had the personality of a cactus. "What I meant was that I would stop at the store and get food and anything else the dog needs. I want to help, even if she can't stay with me."

"We'd better hurry. Lem will be closing up shop, and he doesn't care if it's an emergency. He doesn't reopen for anyone."

"Sounds like you tried?"

"We were having a poker game and ran out of beer. Lem was at the game, so we asked him to restock us. We were going to pay. He wouldn't even reopen for himself."

"Hurry up, then." She'd buy the food and then go back to her rental and go over which property owners her brother had indicated were highly motivated to sell.

"You go in," Danny said. "I'll wait here with Mama. Might need to come up with a better name." He stroked the dog's silky red-brown ears, her fur in crimped-looking waves. The animal sighed in pleasure. Clover could understand that. She'd made nearly the same noise when Danny had used his hands to—

"I'll be back." She did not hurry into the store. She had more dignity than that, and their shared summer was a long time ago. She wasn't that girl anymore.

She came back to the truck with three bags filled with dog paraphernalia, which she was pretty sure she'd been overcharged for. She opened the door to put the loot in the truck.

"My God, woman, did you buy the whole store?" Danny asked as she shoved the bags in.

She stiffened. "I wanted to make sure she had everything she needed."

He rooted in the bags. "A pink rhinestone collar? Lem carries these?"

"Obviously he carries them. Where else would I have gotten it?"

"Well, take it back. I'm not walking a dog with that kind of collar. The one she has just needs to be cleaned up."

"Excuse me?" She couldn't believe what he'd just said. He'd insulted her... She was pretty sure he had.

"I am not putting this collar," he said as he dived into the bags again, "or this leash on Mama. It's not right. She's a ranch dog."

"A ranch dog? You live in a tiny apartment, in a tiny town, not on a ranch."

"I'm not using these." He got out of the truck, lifted down the dog and tied her to the door handle so she was in the shade. Then he strode toward the store. She followed him.

"Danny, the collar and leash are fine. She's a girl."

"She's a ranch dog, and she doesn't need rhinestones." He didn't slow down. She continued after him and back into the store.

"Lem," Danny yelled. "What the hell are you selling? I want a real collar and leash."

"You know the rules," the tall, skinny and stooped Lem said. "No returns."

"That's BS. There are returns when you're selling us crap." Danny glared at the man.

Clover had already guessed she'd been taken advantage of. But she felt it only fair since she was guilty of hitting the dog. Somehow getting gouged made her feel better about that. Like she was paying her dues. "I like the leash and collar." There was that, too.

"Of course you do. You're from New York City," Danny said, as if she'd come from Sodom or Gomorrah.

"They're girlie. And I've spent more of life in Texas than New York."

"They're ridiculous."

"Not man enough to walk a dog sporting a few rhinestones?" she jeered, smiling at the image of him. He was not going to return the darned leash and collar.

"I was man enough for you, darlin'." His tone said exactly what that implied.

She blushed, wanting to smack him because she could see the speculation in Lem's eyes. She did not want to be one of Danny Leigh's women. "That was when you were a bull rider. What are you now? Mayor of a dying town, living off your fading fame." She'd gone too far. She knew it even as the mean words came out. She opened her mouth to apologize or maybe to suck the words back in.

The dog woofed as she came waddling and limping in. She went over to Danny, stretched up and grabbed the leash and collar from his hands, which had fallen to his sides with her ugly words.

Danny seemed to awaken and tried to pull them back. "No," he said. The dog growled and yanked the collar and leash to her, showing teeth.

"Hell's bells, Mayor. That your dog?"

"Just a stray," Danny said. "A bitch who doesn't know what she wants, apparently."

Clover sucked in her breath. Even in their worst teenage fights, Danny had never called her that.

Chapter Three

A call to his sister Jessie had gotten Danny no help and no sympathy for mama dog. His sister had her own child to deal with, her horse therapy program and a husband adjusting to a new job and baby. Jessie had a lot of choice words. Next he tried Lavonda, the sister closest to his age. She said that Cat, her cat, had nixed the idea. Danny told her that he didn't see how a property could function with just a cat to keep the stock in line. Lavonda reminded him who Cat was—an overweight Siamese mix who had a miniature donkey at her beck and call. When she asked him about Clover, he ignored the question.

Mama had made herself at home in a pile of not-so-clean clothes that had missed the hamper. So far she'd been quiet, probably tuckered out. He'd find her a new home soon because even if the original owners came forward, he wasn't giving her up to them. It was obvious they didn't care. His landlord would eventually hear what Danny had in his rooms, and the lease had been clear. No animals. One of those rules he'd figured wouldn't matter because Danny had never planned to stay. It had just been a place to put his gear between competitions. After becoming mayor and retiring from bull riding, he hadn't had time to find a better place. On the other hand, his tiny apartment was convenient to the diner and the rooms were easy for him to clean with his meager housekeeping skills. The rent was cheap, too, freeing up money for his business.

He'd bought properties, purchased more or less as favors to the owners who couldn't keep up with the repairs. The buildings had been sliding toward neglect, so he'd fixed them up, rented them back to the owners at a reasonable price and come up with a grander scheme than just living off rental income and handyman work.

Danny had wanted to buy warehouse properties near to the depot, some of them already broken up into small apartments. He'd also been able to purchase a half dozen buildings on and just behind Miner's Gulch that needed TLC. He'd transform some of them into good housing at a good price. With his ties to bull riding, sisters nearby and friends in Tucson, he'd entice new families to move to Angel Crossing. The town was literally dying, the population aging every day. His homes wouldn't be fancy, but they'd be affordable for couples just starting out. He'd mix in a few more expensive options so that the town didn't get segregated into the haves and have-nots, as he'd seen in many places. After all was said and done, he'd make a little money and the town would be better.

He looked at Mama sleeping peacefully. Maybe he should see about recruiting a vet.

Losing the auction had been a blow to his long-term strategy. He couldn't understand what Clover, or rather her father, wanted to do with the property. He'd searched online for her and found out that she was working for her dad now. He needed to do more checking. He had a vague memory of someone, somewhere in town saying that a New York City company had bought other properties.

He couldn't find anything on Van Camp Worldwide's website about a plan for Arizona. "Why would she buy those old warehouses by the tracks?" he asked the sleeping dog. "They'll have to tear them down. That's what I wanted to do. It was the only way to build anything that would appeal to first-time home buyers. I might have been able to reuse bits and pieces of the interior. Or if I could have found a group of artists, I thought about studios and living spaces. Guess I won't get to do either."

Mama sighed heavily and wiggled her brows before burrowing further into the clothing.

"I'm going to Jim's," he told the dog. He deserved a beer for the day he'd had. A little uncomplicated loving and attention would have been nice, too. Not happening as long as he lived in Angel Crossing. The downside of a small town was that if he made a move on anyone and it didn't work out, he'd have to see her day after day. It had definitely put a damper on his love life.

"Do you really do karaoke on Tuesdays?" Danny asked. He couldn't believe the wood-paneled, domestic-beer-serving tavern ran anything that appealed to someone under the age of 70. He'd seen the sign before but hadn't wanted to ask.

"Country-western only," said Anita, the owner, who'd gotten the place from a former husband.

"Anyone any good?"

"Nah, but that don't stop them." She stared hard at

Danny before going on. "Hear your high school sweetheart's in Angel Crossing."

The gossip nearly had it right. He didn't even wonder about the speed of the stories that flew around town. "She and I dated over a summer when I was with the junior rodeo."

"Makes sense. Couldn't imagine how someone like her went to your high school. She was the rodeo queen or something?"

"Miss Steer Princess," he corrected automatically.

"Huh," Anita said before strolling off.

Danny wondered exactly what of that conversation would be shared. By the time he heard about him and Clover next week, they would have run away as teens to get married in Vegas only to be stopped by a gun-toting daddy. He smiled into his beer. Maybe the story wouldn't be quite that clichéd.

"Mayor," Irvin Miller said as he clapped Danny on the back and sat on the bar stool next to him.

"Mayor," echoed his wife, Loretta. The two dressed alike and even the gray in their hair matched. If you saw one, you always saw the other. Anita served the couple without asking for their order. They always got the same drink: Coors Light draft in a mug that had not been stored in the freezer.

Irvin turned again to Danny after a sip of beer. "We heard that a big company out of New York City is buying up the town."

"The old warehouse buildings by the depot. They were falling down and behind on taxes. It'll be good to see it taken care of."

"It's not just that property. They've bought others and got plans."

"I thought I remembered someone saying that a New York buyer had gotten a couple of places. And what's wrong with having a plan? Angel Crossing could use a little revitalizing," Danny said.

Loretta broke in. "I was at the town hall talking with Pru and she showed me what those Easterners want to do—turn our little metropolis into a resort called Rico Pueblo."

"Resort?" Danny asked. "What the heck is Rico Pueblo?"

Irvin went on. "This VCW company owns a good third of the town already, according to Pru. The plans, though, came in with your lady friend."

"Lady friend? Clover?"

"Yep," Loretta said. "Her. She brought them in and told Pru that her daddy's company wanted to improve Angel Crossing. Pru said your lady friend is asking the town council—" of which Loretta and Irvin were longtime members "—to rezone everything within two blocks of Miner's Gulch into something she's calling an entertainment zone. Everything will have to look a certain way, so they'll tear down almost everything there and rebuild it. Businesses only, though, and that fit into 'an integrated theme highlighting the Western ethos.' We had to look it up and we still don't understand what it means."

"How are they going to get that many businesses? What about everyone already living here or the shops already there?"

Irvin took up the conversation. "Seems that they want to make something like Tombstone or Disneyland but fancier. No showdowns at noon and no saloon girls."

"You'd mention the girls," Loretta said.

Danny couldn't imagine any company wanting to do that with Angel Crossing, but…the land was cheap, and it was within easy driving distance of Tucson and its airport. Was that really why Clover was here?

Irvin added after another sip of beer, "Pru said it'll mean businesses and people will have to move. Not so sure about that."

Maybe the Millers had it wrong about the company taking over the town and driving everyone out. It wouldn't be the first time the couple had gotten only half of a story. "See you, folks," Danny said as he quickly finished his beer and left. He'd just go and see Clover. Find out firsthand what she and VCW meant to do with Angel Crossing.

CLOVER SAT ON her front porch, looking out over the mountains as the sun made its finale. The streaks of purple tonight were a shade she should tell her mother about—not that her mother would care to hear from her. Still, it'd make a beautiful basis for a line of clothing. She sipped at her icy-cold glass of victory beer. She'd gotten another property they needed for this phase and submitted the concept plan to the clerk at the town hall. She'd wanted to wait, preferring not to tip the company's hand for fear of driving up the other properties' prices, but the timeline was tight. To get everything approved by the town, the county and the state in time, the process needed to start now. Actually, it should have started two months ago, but her brother had dropped the ball on that one.

The Rico Pueblo concept of "culturally appropriate" entertainment and retail mixed with residences would transform the town and its economy. There would be jobs and money coming in. It would change Angel Crossing, and for the better—obviously—because right now there wasn't much to recommend the place. Faded facades, uneven sidewalks, potholes on the main street and homes with peeling paint and sagging roofs. She could see the revitalized "downtown" with meandering side streets radiating out to climb into the rugged terrain of the mountains. The residential area would be a combination of time-share rentals and housing managed by VCW. Then in additional phases there would be homes owned by individuals. This was the first project of its kind the company had tried. If they could iron out the kinks, this type of planned community could be used throughout the country. She already had ideas for at least six more venues. She just needed to make the numbers work here.

She nodded to a man walking a dog, which made her think of Mama and her own part in that sad story. Then Danny strolled up the road, stopping to talk with the dog walker. Of course. Because her evening had been going too well. She studied the changes between sixteen-year-old Danny and nearly thirty-year-old Danny—none of which were bad. He'd grown into his height, his shoulders filling out and his gait gaining confidence. Unlike many bull riders she'd seen over the years, he didn't have any hitch in his step or even a visible scar. How had he ridden and won all of those years and come out unscathed? Because he was Danny Leigh.

He turned his head to her almost as if she'd called his name. He smiled. Her heart beat a little faster, just as it always had. Darn it. She was a grown woman, not a naive girl. More important, she had only one reason for being here and that was Rico Pueblo, not reliving a summer love affair.

Her eyes hadn't left Danny, though. He lifted his hat in greeting and stumbled on an uneven bit of street. He righted himself easily, his smile never wavering. If she'd been her vain, beauty-queen self, she would have imagined that she'd made him stumble. Ha!

"Hello, Clover. I heard you were renting Dead Man's Cottage."

"That's very funny."

He came closer. "Really. That's what it's called. The first four owners were hung—one by mistake, the other three for stealing horses or silver."

"Colorful," Clover said, hoping alone at night she wouldn't imagine feeling or seeing the ghosts of the men. "How's Mama?"

"She's settling in. I've got feelers out for a new home for her. It won't be long until my landlord figures out that I've got a dog. But that's not why I'm here."

"Oh?" He was on the narrow porch now, standing over her. She was not intimidated nor interested. She was an MBA-toting businesswoman on her way to running an international corporation.

"I was speaking to Loretta and Irvin Miller. They're on town council, and they told me something intriguing."

"Did they?" She'd hoped her plans would be ignored a little longer, but she was prepared for this situation. She'd studied the town and her father's venture, laying out every scenario and contingency.

"What are you up to? They said you want to tear down the town and rebuild it but restrict what and who can go where."

"Is that what *I'm* doing?"

"Fine. What Van Camp Worldwide is doing. Since your last name is Van Camp, I'd say it was you, too."

"I submitted a concept plan." She didn't need to tell him anything until she was ready.

"Are you trying to ruin my town because I dumped you?"

She couldn't stop the laugh. "I have an MBA from one of the best business schools in the US. I'm in line to become CFO of VCW. Why would I care about a teenage fling?" He stared at her, as if he was expecting her to really answer his question. "You actually believe that? That you dumped me? You must have very different memories than I do."

He crossed his arms over his chest and didn't blink. "I know I didn't call you after that last show. I know you asked about me."

He sounded triumphant. She checked his denim-blue eyes for mischief. Not an iota of levity. He was dead serious. "I was eighteen when we parted ways and on my way to Milan then college," she said, not adding that she'd nearly given up on college to stay with him. She'd been a stupid-in-love girl then. "I never thought about you until I was assigned to come to Angel Crossing."

"I know the 'first time' for a girl is a big deal."

Dear Lord. She definitely remembered their first time. It hadn't been a magical moment and was a memory she'd rather forget. They both had been nervous and inexperienced. The disappointment had been epic. "It must have been a big deal for you, too, since you told anyone who would listen." She sounded snippier than she'd planned. She must still feel a little resentment. Who would have known?

"I apologize for that. My mama taught me better," he said, dropping his arms and dipping his head.

She'd accept his meager apology. "Thank you. It's a little late, though."

"I'd have said it sooner, but my buddies kept ragging on me that a college girl who'd been to Italy wouldn't be interested in a cowboy who was still in high school."

She shrugged and took a sip of beer. He might be right but she still would have liked to have heard from him. To know that she wasn't just some stupid, macho, cowboy conquest. "Would you like a beer?"

Danny hesitated, his blue eyes darkening to something akin to the brightening of a morning sky. "Thank you."

She indicated that he should sit and went in to get him a beer from her limited stock. She'd invited him to have a drink because it was polite. There might be a little bit of the old chemistry. The tingly spark was just an echo of what they'd felt, that intense connection that happened only with a first love. He'd been her first love before he'd been her first lover. She smiled as she thought of their first and only time. His hands had been shaking so badly she'd had to unzip her own jeans.

"Here you are," she said as she handed him the beer and pushed away the old memories. She had a job now. Get the properties VCW needed and convince the town to agree to their rezoning requests and restrictions, which would make Rico Pueblo possible. She couldn't worry about what she'd heard about Danny. That he was starting a rehab and contracting business by buying properties in the same area VCW had slated for its entertainment zone.

He looked at the bottle carefully. "I never pegged you for a beer drinker."

She shrugged. "The label has a horse's head on it."

He took a sip and then said, "You went to Wharton business school? I remember you saying that you wanted to be a designer."

"I thought I wanted to follow in my mother's footsteps. But my talent was more about the numbers and less about creating the perfect hemline. I switched gears partway through my undergrad program. What about you? Weren't you going to go to your mom's alma mater?"

"That was my mom's idea anyway and I tried, but you know what I thought about school. When I started winning big at the bulls and bringing in a decent living, I knew if I went full-time I'd make it."

"I can't imagine your parents were thrilled you quit college." She could imagine her own parents' reaction, if she'd done something like that.

"They just wanted me to be happy. I can always go back to school, with all of the online classes."

She nodded. "I heard you've become a builder or something?"

He talked about his work, then about his family, including his nearly new niece. "Jessie and Payson were so excited when she got pregnant, and now that little Gertie is here, they're awful. Jessie has taken thousands of pictures and sends me all of them. See," he said, passing along his phone with the picture album app open. Clover could hear and see the love he had for the baby. She would never have imagined that of the swaggering cowboy he'd been. Perhaps he really had changed. After all, she had. Being the prettiest girl in the room had stopped being important to her.

"So when are you going to settle down and have babies yourself?" she asked—because it seemed like what she should ask, not because she was dying to know.

"Would need to find the right woman."

Clover refused to think about why she was relieved to hear that.

Danny went on. "What about you or your brother? Any little Van Camps?"

"Knox, well… He's Knox. I'm focused on my career and working with VCW."

"No boyfriend? No fiancé?"

She shook her head. "What about you?"

"Between my business and being mayor, I just don't have the time."

"That doesn't sound like you. You said you could always make time for the ladies."

"I said that in an interview when I was twenty-one and just won a buckle. You kept up with me?"

She may have followed his career…a little. Anyone's first real boyfriend would hold a special spot in their heart. "I lived in Texas. I didn't have much choice but to follow you and everyone else I knew from bull riding."

"Good recovery." He laughed, his blue eyes bright with humor. "I'd better get going. I don't want Mama piddling in the apartment." He unfolded himself from the chair and she stood, too.

"It was good to visit," she said like the Texas beauty queen she'd been.

"Same here." He didn't move and his gaze remained on her.

Clover's breath quickened just a little. That old flush of heat and desire worked its way through her. How could this be, more than ten years after *that* summer? Danny smiled slowly as he put out his hand to shake hers. She grasped it, exquisitely aware of the calluses scraping her palm, making her stomach dance with desire. She pulled her arm a little toward herself, feeling the passion that simmered between them. Danny didn't hesitate but stepped into her, keeping their hands firmly clasped and placing his mouth over hers. Her neck arched and her lips eagerly sought his.

Chapter Four

Cotton candy and popcorn. Clover. The taste of her hadn't changed, taking him back to that summer. The heat and passion, the fear and uncertainty. His hand moved along her familiar and new curves. Every one of them fit into his palm just right, despite the frequent numbness that made the grip in his right hand uncertain. He took one more deep taste of her, then pulled away.

"I've got to go," he said, turning and walking down the hill toward his apartment, where he'd find beer in the fridge and a dog waiting for him.

"Danny Leigh," Clover yelled at him, losing her beauty-queen coolness. "Sticking your tongue down my throat doesn't change anything."

He waved his arm at her without turning.

"Way to go, Mayor," a man standing in his front garden said, giving Danny a thumbs-up.

Danny hadn't meant to kiss Clover. Maybe it was the past sneaking up on him. That was happening a lot since she'd come to town. Even when his friend and riding buddy AJ McCreary had moved to town, Danny's time on the back of a bull had felt far away. He'd been able to put all of that behind him. Between being mayor, rehabbing houses and doing handyman work, he'd been content. He'd been busy—too busy to worry that he didn't have much of a social life. Who needed that when he was so industrious, just like a worker bee. The ladies would always be there, he told himself.

Even better—with his sister Jessie and her husband, Payson, having produced the first grandchild, he was under less pressure to settle down. He could take his time and help his town be its best. Pepper and AJ had started changing Angel Crossing for the better with their community garden and farmers' market. Stylish and affordable housing like he planned would encourage new residents to give the town a try.

Danny walked up the stairs to his small apartment, hoping that he wouldn't find a mess. He ran through people who might want a dog and puppies. He was coming up with a zero. Mama wasn't really big enough to be much of a threat to wild animals or intruders but was too big to be a lapdog. She was an awkward size and who knew what the puppies were.

Mama waddled to him as soon as he got in the door. The apartment looked as neat as it ever did. He put a blanket over her to hide what he was carrying in case someone squealed to his landlord. He carried the wiggling animal down the stairs and through the back lot, past the restaurant's Dumpster. Once they reached a patch of low scrub, he put her down. The grass nearly hid her and her rhinestone collar and leash. She sniffed and quickly got down to business. He'd brought along a bag and would throw away what he had to in the Dumpster. She sat down, tired out from the very short walk. She couldn't be too long from delivery, he thought. He vaguely recollected one of their dogs having puppies as a kid, but he only remembered how cute they were, not the lead up or the process of them being born. He'd call his folks for advice. Maybe they would want a dog to go with them on their travels. Plus, they had a ton of friends. One or more of them might want a puppy.

He carried the dog back to the apartment, where he fed her and gave her clean water. Then he dialed his parents and left a message.

He took a beer from his fridge and sat in his tiny living room with his laptop open and the TV on the Bull Riding Network. He rubbed at his numb fingers, the ones the doctor told him might regain feeling or not. Sometimes he was sure they were better. Then he'd go to pick up a glass and drop it. Still, he'd retired. He'd refused to regret that it had been an "injury" that took him out, not that he'd told anyone that. When he'd said he was retiring because he wanted to go out on top, none of his friends had questioned him.

"Friends in Low Places" sang out from his phone. It was an old riding buddy who was watching the same competition on TV. They were both sitting this one out—Danny because he was retired and Frank because he'd reinjured his foot. Danny was on beer three when they said goodbye. He considered going to bed and taking Mama out for her final potty break before the long night. Maybe one more beer then bed? Good idea.

He finished his longneck and went to get himself another, liking this slightly floating feeling. He was completely relaxed, not worrying about the dog—who really needed a new name—about his town or about Clover. Dang it. Her taste and curves popped back into his mind, and he tried to focus on the TV.

By the time the contest and another beer were done, he was ready for bed. First he'd take the dog out one last time. He didn't want any accidents. Dang, it was a pain having a dog in a second-floor apartment. Fortunately, because it was dark and late, he didn't need to bundle her up and carry her down the stairs. He could lead her with her sparkly leash. He went down the steps, the floating feeling continuing as he stumbled over a stone or two. Definitely time for this cowboy to hit the hay. Mama did her business fast. Danny started back to the apartment.

He got to the bottom of the stairs and Mama scrabbled toward the top, pulling on the leash. Danny meant to let go but his numb fingers didn't work as well as they should and she jerked on his arm as he stepped up, pulling him off balance. Danny face-planted on the stairs and saw stars. He cursed as the dog darted to the top and barked at him.

He lay sprawled on the stairs, glad no one was nearby. He needed to catch his breath and check for damage. Not much. More pride than anything. He pushed himself up and Mama barked.

"Jutht a minute." *What the hell?* He used his tongue to explore the hole at the front of his mouth. Son of a— The fall had knocked out the fake tooth he'd gotten as a kid after a spectacular crash on his minibike. Great. Nothing he could do tonight. He walked slowly up the stairs, the pain from the fall and the throbbing in his mouth telling him tomorrow morning would not be fun. Hell. He was a bull rider. *Retired* bull rider. Still, he'd lived through worse.

"Inthide, Mama," he said and opened the door. She scooted past him and sat on the floor, fluffy tail wagging, waiting for her treat and the leash to come off. "Proud of yourthelf?" The dog barked. Wait till she had to eat generic food because he had to spend all of his money on a new tooth.

Maybe Clover would buy some of the expensive brand she'd bought at Lem's—but, no, he wasn't asking her for anything. They'd been a summer-lovin' teen thing. They were adults and she'd already messed with his plans, just like she had that summer. He wasn't getting stupid over her again. He'd learned a lot since their time together. He wouldn't be showing her exactly what he'd learned, though. At best they were Angel Crossing–style neighbors. At worst, they were businesspeople on opposite sides of the fence.

He gave Mama a treat, took an aspirin and lay down in his sagging bed that nearly filled the room. He really needed to move. As soon as he got more properties sold and had a little cash, he'd find his own place and redo it the way he wanted. What he had now was good enough. The bed dipped under Mama's weight and she dug at the covers as he moved his legs to accommodate her. He shouldn't let her on the bed, but he was too tired to make her get down.

"Don't have puppyth," he told her as he settled into his pillow, "pleathe."

She sighed deeply and scooted to take up more of the bed.

CLOVER USED HER confident pageant walk to get her across the threshold and into Jim's Tavern, the only bar in town. She wanted to check it out and determine if it was the kind of kitschy business that would appeal to the Rico Pueblo clientele. Her father had said he'd prefer buying up everything and starting over. Clover, however, had outlined an approach that would purchase properties and work with current business owners so VCW could best leverage its investment— that was what she'd told her father, anyway.

Few patrons glanced Clover's way. Instead, they were glued to the stage and the two women laughing their way through a country duet. Neither could sing but they didn't care. The crowd was with them, laughing along and clapping. Actually, most of the crowd was women… Not most. *All* of the patrons were women and there was a woman behind the bar. Now, this was interesting. Not what Clover had expected. That seemed to be the case again and again in Angel Crossing.

"Whoa! Clover," said the tall light-haired woman with the karaoke microphone in her hand. "Come up here. You can sing a lot better than us. Sing that song you did when you were named Miss Steer Princess? 'God Bless the USA.'"

Clover looked harder at the cowgirl who was motioning her forward and the short dark-haired woman beside her. Danny's sisters. The two women had been on the road with their brother back when Clover had been the princess. She'd had an okay voice because her mother insisted she take lessons.

Lavonda chimed in, "Or you could sing 'It's Raining Men.'"

She'd sung that song during a rain delay at a rodeo. Of course Lavonda would remember that. Clover didn't want to humiliate herself but she could go along with the suggestion to get a few brownie points from the women of Angel Crossing. She'd need allies. Clover walked with purpose and grace to the open area set aside for the singing.

"Whoop, whoop," Jessie said. "This'll be a treat."

"Anything's better than the two of you," a woman heckled. Jessie and Lavonda laughed.

Clover smiled at the audience of women. They actually looked friendly.

"We cued up the song," Lavonda said, her dark eyes and hair so different from her light-haired older sister's. "Good to see you again." Then the smaller woman leaned forward and whispered quietly, "Heard you've been visiting with Danny. What's that about, huh?"

Clover just smiled. The speed at which gossip zipped through a small town shouldn't be a surprise. Who needed newspapers or TV when there was such an efficient way to pass along information?

Jessie and Lavonda went back to their bar stools, and Clover sang. She'd forgotten how much fun it was to perform. She hammed it up for the audience and got talked into singing another two songs before giving up the mic. She was parched. The Leigh sisters motioned for her to join them. She wanted to say no, but there was no polite way to bow out. Plus, the two of them might give her more insight into the town and what the mayor had planned.

"What do you want? We're buying," Lavonda said. Jessie stayed silent. She'd always been the quiet one.

"A beer."

"Anita, a beer for the best performer of the night."

Jessie took a drink. "You in town to buy it?"

"Something like that," Clover said. There was no use lying. Everyone had heard about her buying the warehouses at the end of Miner's Gulch, plus other properties. When Rico Pueblo opened, she would re-name the street Torro Boulevard.

"My husband, Jones, and I are curious about your plans," Lavonda said with a pleasant smile. "We own a guide company and more people visiting here would certainly be great for our finances. But this area is eco-logically fragile. There are archaeological sites nearby that need to be protected, too."

Clover hadn't known about any sites. There hadn't been any noted on any of the surveys or maps. "There are?" she asked noncommittally.

"Jones has been exploring. He's an archaeologist."

Clover nodded, waiting for more from Lavonda.

"Talk about that another time," Jessie said. "I want to hear what Clover's been up to, besides being a busi-ness mogul."

Clover tried to understand what Jessie was really asking and decided to take her at face value. She gave them the short version. "What about you?" she asked Jessie when she'd finished her short bio. "Still riding, even with the baby?"

"Not the trick riding," Jessie said. "Gave that up, but I have a therapeutic horse-riding program for young-sters. Kids with physical and emotional challenges."

Lavonda added, "Don't get her started on Gertie. We're out so that she can live it up and act like a nor-mal human being."

Jessie gave her sister a dirty look, the kind of sib-ling communication Clover always wanted to have with Knox and didn't.

Lavonda said, "This is the first time Jessie has gone

out on her own since Gertie made her grand entrance. That girl already has the flair for the dramatic."

"She does?"

"Yes," Lavonda said, shushing her sister. "Jessie's husband is a pediatric surgeon, operated on thousands of kids, probably. When Gertie made her appearance at their ranch—Jessie kept saying the pain wasn't bad enough to go to the hospital—he fainted. Smacked down on the floor. The three of them shared an ambulance."

"Stop telling that story. That's not the way it happened," Jessie said. "Payson didn't faint. He tripped."

"He tripped because he was faint."

"Faint because he hadn't eaten or slept."

The sisters bantered back and forth for a few minutes before returning to their interrogation.

"Bet you were surprised that Danny is mayor, huh?" Lavonda asked.

"He was a popular rider," Clover said flatly.

"Popular with you," Jessie mumbled, sounding suddenly unfriendly.

"We were very young."

"You're older by a couple of years, aren't you?" Jessie asked without a hint of humor.

"I don't remember," Clover lied.

"Really?" Jessie's sage-green gaze locked on to Clover. "Never knew a woman who forgot her first—"

"Danny is our baby brother," Lavonda broke in. "We might feel a little protective."

"He's a grown man," Clover reminded them. "I don't think he'd appreciate you discussing his...private life."

"Sorry about that. Like Lavonda said, he's our baby brother."

"He's lucky to have you two," she said, meaning it. Nothing like her and Knox. They had shuttled between their separated parents until Knox settled with their dad in New York and she chased tiaras with her mother in Texas.

Lavonda smiled and said, "He'll probably disown us…again…if you tell him we talked to you. So could we just keep this between us hens?" Jessie nodded agreement.

"Sure," Clover said. "One thing, though. Why did Danny agree to be mayor? He won't tell me."

"That's his story," Jessie said, "and it's time I head back to my baby. Come on, Lavonda."

"I'm proud of you. I expected us to leave at least an hour ago."

Clover watched the sisters stand and said, "It was good seeing you, and your secret is safe with me."

"Wait—one more thing," Lavonda said as Jessie gave her an impatient look. "This isn't a warning or anything. Danny is different than when he was a teen, but one thing that hasn't changed is how much he… cared for you when you were young."

Before Clover could respond, the women walked away. What did they mean by that? Danny had some torch for her? But they said to leave him alone? The bonds between siblings made her envious and confused. She didn't understand exactly how it all worked.

Time to finish her beer and head home. The chat with Danny's sisters hadn't been anything more than a little girl talk. A lot of water and everything else had passed under the bridge since Danny and she had been a couple. He might be a better kisser and had aged well. That didn't mean anything more than that she'd been working too hard and neglecting her social life. She'd take care of that as soon as this project got off the ground.

She'd spend her time reworking her numbers and tweaking her presentation for the council. She planned to win over this town and prove to her father she was the kind of executive he needed. Not much at all riding on this upcoming meeting, where she'd be laying it on the line in front of an old boyfriend who could still make her forget her name when they kissed.

Chapter Five

As he waited for the town-council meeting to start, Danny's tongue pushed at the empty space between his teeth. The dentist required payment up front and Danny was a little short. He'd been desperate enough to look on the ground around the stairs for the knocked-out tooth but he hadn't found it. He'd been nodding along to the conversation, not opening his mouth and holding his lip down over the gap. He'd never thought of himself as vain, but a big old hole in his mouth made him want to hide.

Of course, Clover, in a professional but formfitting suit, sat front and center in the audience at the council meeting. Her proposal was number two on the agenda, after the Pledge of Allegiance. He looked around at the four other members of the board. They'd called Angel Crossing home all of their lives, and like a lot of the old-timers, they didn't want their town to change. But they also understood that without change their children and grandchildren would never stay. He had a vague idea of how they might view Van Camp Worldwide's proposal. He'd been explaining his own ideas, but they were long-term solutions, not the quick one that Clover would be presenting.

The president of the board looked at his watch and hammered down the gavel. "Let's get this show on the road. I want to be home before that dancing program starts. Everyone stand for the Pledge."

Danny stood, turned to the flag and caught the gleam of Clover's auburn hair out of the corner of his eye. He would not be distracted by her or the memories of their recent kiss.

"Miss Van Camp," said Bobby Ames, the president of the board and Angel Crossing's lone attorney and taxidermist. "Your presentation, please. You have ten minutes."

Clover stood and picked up a stack of printouts. She quickly went down the table handing out the colorful and slick paper. Danny would not feel bad that he hoped her big-city presentation raised the hackles on his fellow board members.

"I am here on behalf of Van Camp Worldwide," Clover started.

"We know that, missy. Get to the point. What do you want us to do for you?"

She looked a little flustered, but her smile seemed genuine. "It's more what we can do for you all," she said, a Texas twang suddenly entering her voice, making her sound more like the girl he'd met on the junior rodeo circuit.

"Give everyone a job and a thousand dollars," Loretta Miller said.

"I wish I could help y'all out."

Boy, she was laying it on thick. Didn't she know that Arizona wasn't Texas?

"Seven minutes," Bobby said.

Clover took in a long breath and stood with regal,

beauty-queen posture. "Van Camp Worldwide can provide the town with a viable plan to transform it into a new style of resort that will bring both jobs and tax revenue."

"That's what they all say," Loretta muttered to Irvin.

"The materials I've provided outline in detail our proposal." She went on before Bobby could interrupt her with another time check. "We will and have purchased properties at fair market price, but I'm before this body because we need to secure permission to rezone the Miner's Gulch corridor and demolish the properties from just north of the town hall to the railroad."

"Wait," Danny interrupted. He had properties along Miner's Gulch. He needed the zoning to remain as is for his own plan to work. He'd already sunk a chunk of his savings into his own revitalization project. She'd messed up part of his plan when she'd purchased the warehouse properties. "I talked with everyone about what I wanted to do. I'll use local labor and end up with affordable housing for residents—a mix of senior, family and singles. It's just what we need."

"When you have your plan ready to present formally, bring it in," Bobby said. "You really shouldn't even comment on Rico Pueblo."

"But I'm mayor," Danny said, not looking at Clover. "I live here and I care about Angel Crossing. I won't come in and cut out its heart, pull out my profits and move along."

"That's not how the law works," Clover said, her

drawl disappearing again. "I can have a lawyer come with me next time, if need be."

"No need for that," Bobby said. "I'm a lawyer and I know what we're mucking into. Mayor, we can't make a decision that favors you because you're 'local.'"

"Why the hell not?" Loretta asked.

"President Ames," Clover said, her drawl rounding out her words. "Thank you for being so fair-minded about the concept plan. If you turn to page eight, you'll see our projections for tax revenue going forward. I believe that sort of influx will be essential for the smooth operation of—"

Danny interrupted, "But it'll cost us in police and maintenance. Think of all of the people here to party. Chief Rudy and his team are stretched to breaking just keeping up with the current population."

"Mayor," Bobby warned.

Clover went on, speaking directly to him. "The additional revenue from taxes plus the private and state-of-the art security measures will not put any more strain on the town's finances than the current situation. That is outlined on page thirty-six."

When they were teens all Clover had talked about was her hair and the sorority she'd pledge when she went to college. Where had she hidden this Clover? He scanned quickly through her material. "Wait a minute," he said. "What's this about tax forgiveness and stepped-down assessment and an amusement-tax abatement?"

"Thank you, Mayor—a very insightful question," she said sweetly, like doubly sweet sweet tea. "This front-end investment by the community will match that of Van Camp Worldwide's, making Rico Pueblo a public-private partnership."

"I thought you said you'd be giving us revenue," one of the other council members said, followed by similar questions.

There. He'd gotten her. They'd have to say no to her, which would be a yes for him when he gave his plan. Not that he really had any doubt. He'd been living in Angel Crossing and had settled in for the long haul.

The council members moved from asking about revenue on to how they would deal with the snow…if they got any this year. At this elevation, they did get the white stuff, but they were also in the high desert, so they didn't get a lot of precipitation, period.

"Mr. President," Clover said, her voice easily carrying over the continued discussions. "I hate to be pushy about this, but you see, we have deadlines to meet with the state."

"We won't be bullied," Danny said, sounding self-righteous and thinking that was just the right tone.

"I'm not trying to put the pressure on, Mayor Leigh. It's just that those are our deadlines. If we don't make them, then we'll have to pull the project. There's another location just a few miles closer to Tucson that actually might work better. I told the board at VCW, though, that Angel Crossing had the heart to be the kind of community we want. Plus, there were hard-working men and women who would be proud to be our employees."

Danny saw the faces of his fellow council members. They were eating it up. Couldn't they see she was playing them? "Really. Another town but we were the top pick. Isn't that a convenient detail to bring out now? We don't need your kind of attention. I already have a plan to put Angel Crossing on the map. A charity bull-riding event featuring all the top cowboys. I'll even come out of retirement for this one." There. See if she could top that.

Her blue eyes narrowed and bright pink stained her cheeks. "You just came up with that. You don't have a competition organized," she said, hanging on to her twang but glaring at him.

"Are you calling me a liar?" He kept his gaze locked on her. She wasn't going to win this. It was his town and his future.

"Hot damn," Bobby said. "A bull-riding competition. You shouldn't keep events like that under your hat, Mayor. Wish we could get into all of the details tonight. We'll talk about it at our next meeting."

"What about me?" Clover asked, her smile a little less bright.

"Next month for you, too."

"That puts us awfully close to our deadline. We'd certainly be willing to underwrite the cost of a special meeting, if need be."

Bobby looked at the wall clock pointedly. "Our next meeting. We should be able to give you an answer then. Anyone else?"

Irvin piped up. "This rodeo is going to be bigger than that time the governor's car broke down and I gave him a ride back to Tucson."

"Is AJ helping?" asked Claudette, the fourth council member and receptionist at the town's clinic.

Danny stalled. "He's so busy with Santa Faye Ranch." His friend and fellow retired bull rider would probably help, when Danny asked. Of course, that would mean actually organizing the event, which he'd never done before. Why had he let Clover get to him like that?

"We expect a full report next month, Mayor," Bobby said sternly with his *Law & Order* lawyer voice.

Danny felt nothing but relief when Bobby moved along on the agenda. What was he doing? He'd always been focused, always been able to make a list of what he wanted to accomplish and then check off each item. Not now. Not since he'd really understood his retirement was permanent.

"We're adjourned." Bobby slammed the gavel. Clover shot across the room, trying to talk to Bobby, who waved her off. He was nearly running from the building, intent on his dancing show. The other council members listened to Clover. Danny didn't move, not sure if he wanted to speak with her or not.

CLOVER KNEW SHE was intelligently answering the council members who came up to speak with her. At the same time, she was aware of Danny standing to her left. Watching with his blue gaze and arms crossed over his chest. He looked just like a cowboy waiting to confront the black-hatted bad guy in a Western. In classes at Wharton, they hadn't discussed how to face a former lover/boyfriend during business negotiations. Maybe she should call the dean of the school and suggest that class.

"I understand your concerns," she said to Irvin. "I will take that into consideration."

"See that you do," the older man said just before he was led away by the woman who was obviously his wife.

"Mayor," the woman named Claudette said as she walked toward the door, "we're going over to Jim's. You coming?"

Clover kept her gaze on her large professional rolling case packed with papers.

"Not tonight," he said. Clover moved, but not quite fast enough. Danny reached out and took her arm. "Need to ask you a few questions, Ms. Van Camp." His voice would easily carry to the leaving council members and she wondered if anyone else had noticed that he'd suddenly developed a lisp.

She stopped, not afraid or worried, but tell that to the quiver in the pit of her stomach. "Certainly, Mayor Leigh. I'm happy to answer any of your questions, though you might want to wait until my next presentation."

"Since you're trying to run me out of business and change my town, I think I'll ask you now."

"Certainly." She used her polite smile. She'd dealt with caterers and venue owners for her mother. Danny would be much easier than them. She knew him, or had known him. Wouldn't that give her an advantage?

His gaze stayed stern and locked on her even as he uncrossed his arms. "I'm going to ask you again—why Angel Crossing?"

He still thought this was about revenge for a teenage affair she'd forgotten long before she'd graduated from college. "VCW did a survey of properties and locations in a radius of major airports with appropriate transportation connections and with land at favorable pricing. Angel Crossing met the criteria."

"Really?"

"Really. Danny, my brother headed the project initially."

"Then you stepped in."

"Yes, I did. Knox hadn't—" She stopped herself, calculating how much she should say. "He was called to another project." That wasn't a lie. He was on another project but because he'd messed this one up.

"How, with all of the tax breaks and waiving of fees, can this provide revenue for Angel Crossing?" Danny asked, obviously changing tack.

"I explained it in the presentation. This may require short-term pain for all of us with the opportunity for long-term gain."

"Seems like we're the only ones in for 'short-term pain.'"

"VCW will be investing in land and improvements before any money comes in." He snorted. "What?" she asked, beginning to get annoyed.

"Your daddy's company doesn't do anything for nothing."

"Of course not. We wouldn't be in business if we didn't make money."

"Exactly. There's something you're not telling us in these papers." He waved his copy of her presentation.

"I'm not lying," she said. That accusation really hurt.

"Everybody lies. Didn't you lie to me?"

"What are you talking about?"

"You said it didn't matter that I was just a bull rider from a family who followed the rodeo. It mattered all right. I was just a notch in your sorority belt." His arms crossed his chest again and his eyes had gone an icy blue.

None of this should matter. They'd been teens. It'd been years ago, and had they really made any promises to each other? "What about you? Telling all of your friends? Bragging that you'd...well, you know."

His shoulders drooped a little. "I do apologize for that. What can I say? I was young."

They had been young, so young. "You didn't email or call."

He dropped his arms and shoved his hands into his pockets. Her heart clenched. He did that when he was embarrassed or uncomfortable. She was transported right back to the first time he'd asked her out.

"My friends told me that you'd moved on, you know. You were going to Italy, then on to college."

Her mother had dragged her to Milan for a crash course in fashion because Clover was expected to work on her degree and spend time at Cowgirl's Blues. "My mom and school kept me busy. You said you had no fear or something like that."

"That was about getting onto the back of a bull." He pushed his hands harder into his pockets. "Going after an older woman was something else. When you didn't even send me a postcard, I figured you'd met some sophisticated Italian guy. Probably a prince or duke or something."

She laughed loudly. "The men in Milan told me—the two or three who actually spoke English—that I was an unsophisticated girl. Beauty-pageant pretty was nothing to them. Talk about a wake-up call." She should be embarrassed to reveal such a failure on her part, but it felt comfortable with Danny, in an odd way.

"Those guys were blind," he said, taking his hands out of his pockets.

"It's fine. They were right. I was unsophisticated, and I thought I was *Vogue* pretty. I'm not."

"You're better. You're *real* pretty." His gaze locked on hers and she saw he was sincere.

"Thank you," she said with difficulty. It had taken her years to learn to take a compliment without pointing out all of her flaws. "You were really a nice boy then."

"Then?"

"I don't know you now."

"You could," he said.

"Stop. I don't want Danny, champion bull rider who all of the women love. I'm good with Danforth Leigh," she said and meant it.

"What about you? Are you still Clover Anastasia Van Camp?"

"Yes, a part of me. But a bigger part is plain old Clover, the woman with an MBA and a way with numbers."

"Good to meet you, plain old Clover."

She smiled at him, thinking that she was glad they'd cleared the air of the past. It had been silly to hang on to that hurt. "So what happened to you? How did you lose the tooth? I couldn't figure out why you were lisping until just now."

His hands went back into his pockets. "Fell." He barely moved his lips.

"Must have been some fall to knock out a tooth."

"It was a fake tooth. I knocked it out the first time when I was a kid."

"Riding?"

"Kind of. I had a minibike and thought I'd try jumping over two dogs and a goat. It didn't go as well as I'd planned." His smile looked odd because he still didn't show the empty space where the tooth had been.

A bit of silence stretched between them. "Guess I'll see you around."

"Guess so. This doesn't mean that I don't think your plan is bad."

"I've got a month to convince you otherwise."

"You ready to leave? I'll escort you out."

She felt the whiplash of being thrown back to those faraway days when Danny acted like a "pardon me, ma'am" cowboy. He was back and it still made her heart flutter. She needed to stop that right in its tracks. "I'm a grown woman with pepper spray and big-city experience. I'll be fine."

He just looked at her and waited for her to precede him. She wouldn't allow him to follow her home. She needed to wrest back control. She didn't want to feel like the helpless little woman. She'd given up that role years ago.

"My car is there." She pointed. "I know you want to meet up with your friends."

"They'll wait." He didn't move. Again, she was older, wiser. She would not cause a scene. She walked with purpose to her car, started it up and waved as she pulled out. Danny stood watching her drive away. She couldn't decide how that made her feel. Then she told herself the only feeling she had was satisfaction from settling their ancient and very personal hurts—no matter the recent kiss. Now she could move forward on strictly professional footing.

Chapter Six

Danny amazed himself. Maybe he should give up on being a builder and become a charity ride event promoter or organizer or whatever because he'd organized the hell out of the first annual Save Angel Crossing (SAC) Bull-Riding Extravaganza. He had the date booked at the community college's arena, he'd gotten two of his old sponsors to put up cash to help with advertising costs and prizes, and he'd called ten of his former riding buddies and all ten had said hell yes. He'd roped (he was getting good at puns) AJ into talking to a stock contractor. The goal was to get the animals for free or, at worst, a huge discount. Of course, Danny had had to tell everyone he would be competing. They said that would draw the crowds. "A 'champeen' back in the saddle."

"You sure about this, buddy?" AJ asked during another call for this damned charity ride that had taken over every one of Danny's waking hours—not spent working on properties or dealing with Maggie May—as he'd decided to call Mama—or fantasizing about Clover.

"Why wouldn't I be sure? Two years isn't long. Plus, you're getting easy bulls, right?"

"Ha. Dave said he wants to try out new stock, ones that he's sure will be in the money. He figures this is a way to get them a name, reputation."

"What the—"

"Cowboys who want things for free can't be choosy," AJ said.

"Yeah, well, *farmers* and their significant others who will benefit from a charity bull ride should look out for the guy who is making it happen." Danny had decided once he got the event rolling that any money they made (which was still not a sure thing) would go to the community garden project and the rehab of the old theater into an under-roof farmers' market.

"You offered," AJ said. "Besides, you'll draw in more riders and spectators with challenging bulls. You know that."

He did know that. He also knew that his hand and sometimes part of his arm went from sort-of to totally numb without warning. "Since you're so excited about these bulls, I'll expect you to talk the two new champs into coming."

There was a long silence and finally AJ said, "I'll do it, but it's for Pepper. Gotta go. I've got llama training."

"What?"

"The yarn from the llamas isn't as popular, so we're going to train them to carry packs and rent them out for hikes."

"That's just wrong in so many ways."

"They've got to earn their keep," AJ said and hung up.

So, Danny had no choice. He'd have to get back to bull-rider training and do it fast. Until he could be sure about his arm, he didn't want to ask AJ to help him find a practice bull. Angel Crossing didn't have a gym but that was no excuse for not getting into riding shape.

Best to get on this now. Waiting would mean he might talk himself out of it. Danny searched online for new ideas and workout routines that he could do without special equipment. There was one that used a balance ball—something about working on his core by standing on the unsteady ball. He found a basketball at the back of his closet. He needed to balance for fifteen minutes at a time to get the maximum benefit.

He found a rerun of one of his PBR championship rides to watch. Perfect. He should analyze what he would need to do to compete against his friends—friendly competition or not.

"Time to get in shape," he told the empty living room. He put one foot on the ball. Good. Then he transferred his weight to the leg on the ball and everything went south faster than a Texas two-step. His arms pinwheeled as the ball slid from under his foot. He overcorrected, flew forward, twisting his body until his head connected solidly with the edge of the TV stand. He yelled.

On his back on the floor, Danny noticed that more than a few flies had gone to the great beyond in the ceiling's light fixture. Maggie May whined and nudged his ear with her cold, wet nose. Ugh. His head hurt but he didn't have a concussion. He knew about those. He needed to get up and ice his head to keep the throbbing from turning into a goose egg.

Why couldn't he have just done old-fashioned sit-ups to strengthen his core? What the hell kind of idea was it to stand on a damned ball? He sat up. No dizziness, so he stood. Blood dripped onto his jeans. Damn. He ached in other places now that he was upright. He pulled up his T-shirt and held it against his head. He'd better not need stitches. He couldn't afford that on top of the tooth that needed to be repaired. The butterfly bandages in the cabinet would have to do.

In the bathroom mirror, he saw the cut, high on his head, was a mess of bloody hair and ragged skin. Dang it. Good thing it was Saturday and he didn't have any work. He looked at the cut again. He needed his hair trimmed or he'd never get the butterfly bandages to stick. He considered using his razor, but even he knew dragging a sharp blade along the open ends of the wound would be a dumb move. Plus, he'd have to do it backward in the mirror.

AJ. His friend would have clippers. They had to use something like that on the llamas and alpacas at the ranch. AJ would also keep his mouth shut if Danny asked. Probably. Before he could talk himself out of it, he called.

"What do you want now? Bulls that have been broke to a saddle?" AJ asked instead of saying "Hey."

"Can you get away and come into town?"

"I told you I'm working with the llamas."

"Right. Well—" Hell. What would he do now?

"What's wrong?"

"I fell."

"From a bull?"

"Sure. I dragged a bull up to my apartment."

"If you fell, call 911 or drive to the ER in Tucson."

"No way," Danny said. "This isn't worth their time.

I just need you to clip away the hair. Scissors won't get close enough and I can't shave it."

"Fine. Come on out to the ranch. You owe me, though, especially since I'm guessing you don't want to involve Pepper."

Danny was proud that he'd come up with such an easy and cheap solution. AJ would clip his hair so the cut could be bandaged. He looked down at his bloodstained T-shirt and picked up another almost clean shirt from a pile. Now he needed ice to keep the pounding to a bongo-drum level.

He walked into his little kitchen and heard whimpering from Maggie May, who'd wedged herself into the small closet where he kept cleaning supplies, including rags—which had become her nest—along with discarded shoes she'd pushed out of her way. The dog was licking at…a puppy. He looked down at Maggie May, who seemed proud of her accomplishment. The pup was coal black except for a pink nose, a white toe on the left front paw and a spot of white on one ear. Cute little critter. It squeaked and squawked as Maggie May nudged and cleaned him. Danny couldn't leave the dog. He called AJ and told him about the puppies. His friend agreed to drive into town with his clippers.

DANNY SAT AGAINST the fridge watching the dog. Enough time passed that he had refilled his towel with ice. His skin was nice and numb but a headache was building. He hoped AJ got here soon because the wound just wouldn't stop bleeding. Maggie May yipped loudly and he scooted back to her. The first puppy lay close to his mother and Danny expected to see another little wiggling body. Nothing. Maggie May's sides heaved and she whined. He had no idea if this was normal or not. He reached out to pet her and she snapped at him. She must be in pain. She yipped loudly and then barked. He looked—no puppy. And no sign of a puppy.

Should he call Clover? They'd taken care of the dog together and it seemed like something bad was happening. The dog's side rippled with what he assumed was a contraction. His head was throbbing in time with the movement.

"Maggie May," he murmured, slowly reaching out his hand to see if she would allow him to touch her. She raised her lip over her teeth but didn't growl. Laying his hand on her side, he could feel the contractions. He petted her slowly until his hand was on her hindquarters so he could move her tail out of the way.

Dang. It looked bad, her legs smeared with blood and gummy pink wetness. Could Pepper help with this? He moved as Maggie May barked loudly and the door shook with a knock. Good. That was AJ. He'd owned dogs. Maybe he'd have an idea of what they should do.

Danny got to his feet, the pain in his head peaking as Maggie M whimpered. "We'll get you help, sweetheart," he said, hurrying to the door, the nearly melted ice still clutched to his head.

"AJ," Danny said before the door was fully open.

"Jeez, Danny. Are you trying to reenact *The Texas Chainsaw Massacre*?" Pepper asked as she entered the apartment.

Before Danny could say anything, AJ broke in. "She caught me with clippers and bandages. She knew I was lying when I said it was nothing."

The dog yowled.

"What the heck is that?" Pepper asked.

"Maggie May. She's having her puppies and I think one's stuck. Can you check her first?" Danny asked, relieved that Pepper was there.

"You," she said, pointing to Danny, "sit down. AJ, take one of the pads from my bag and press it hard on his thick skull."

"Hey—" Danny started.

"No use arguing when she's got that tone. That's her 'physician's assistant Pepper in charge' look, too. Don't fight it, man."

"Let's have a look… Lordy be," Pepper said.

"What?" Danny asked, surging to his feet. Had the dog died? Had the puppy died?

"Sit down before you fall down," Pepper said with authority. "Everything is fine. While we were talking Maggie May here got down to business. There are three puppies."

"Three? Wow."

"I don't think we're done. I feel one more."

"Four puppies. Oh, crap. How are we going to find homes for all of them?"

"Sit so I can push this really hard on the cut," AJ said. "You know that our daughter is on a girls' weekend with her Grana and Grammy C. Pepper and I had planned a whole weekend alone together. You're lucky I answered the phone."

"Sorry, man," Danny mumbled. His bull-riding buddy had settled nicely into family life with his daughter and Pepper. The two hadn't announced when the wedding was but it couldn't be far off.

"This looks like it's going to need more than butterflies. How did you do it?"

Danny tried to think of a lie but his brain felt mushy

between the ache of the cut and his worry for Maggie May. "I should probably have called Clover."

"Really?" AJ asked as he pressed the bandage back on the wound.

Danny saw stars as the pain went from throb to spike. "She helped rescue her," he rasped.

"Ahh," AJ said.

"What?"

"Nothing."

"It's something."

"Nah. Just remembering the two of you from back when. Attached at the hip—and lips—that whole summer."

"We were young," Danny said. "She's got a New York life now." He hoped that would end the conversation.

"Four puppies," Pepper said, ending AJ's unwelcome comments. "Three boys and one girl. Now I'll check you. AJ, get the suture kit."

Danny might be a big bad bull rider, but he'd never liked getting stitches. He wiggled in the chair, trying to get his brave on. "How many do you think?"

"A few," Pepper said. "I'll numb it up." She patted his shoulder as she looked at the wound. "Get the clippers, too, AJ. I'm going to have to shear him before I start."

CLOVER STOOD ON the wooden steps at the back of the diner that led up to Danny's small apartment. She hesitated even though she had a very valid reason for stopping by. She'd heard about the puppies and his stitches. She was only interested in the canines. She felt responsible for Mama. If she hadn't hit her with the car, though, the creature would probably have given birth out in the open. *What a way to justify hitting a dog, Clover.*

She moved before she had a chance to talk herself out of the visit. She knocked. A "woof" came from inside. She didn't hear any movement that sounded human. She waited. She knocked again. More barking. What if Danny had passed out? What if he'd landed on Mama and she and her puppies were trapped under him? No, that wasn't likely since the dog was barking.

Clover tried the door. Most people in Angel Crossing didn't lock up during the day. The handle turned. She opened it, yelling out for Danny as she walked in. Nobody other than Mama and the puppies.

The mother dog raced past Clover and outside. Nuts. The puppies mewled and cried. Clover took in their fat, wriggling bodies, then turned to look out the door. Mama was at the bottom of the stairs sniffing around the small parking lot. She probably just needed to go potty, but Clover wasn't going to take a chance on the dog staying away from car wheels. How would she explain it to Danny? *I broke into your apartment, let your dog out and she got hit...again.* She went down the stairs and stood by Mama as she took care of business. Back inside, the dog quickly settled back into her box with her puppies.

Clover was surprised by the number of little animals. They were all so different looking. Brown, black, white, spotted. Their coats went from smooth to rough to curly to long and silky. She couldn't imagine what sort of dog had fathered them. Clover leaned over the box, reaching out to touch the white one, who looked to be the smallest.

"What the hell are you doing?" Danny asked with fierce anger.

"Oh," Clover said, snatching back her hand and whirling to face him. "Jeez Louise," she gasped, trying to take in his half-shaved head and raw wound. And he was sunburned.

He closed the door to the bedroom and took two large steps toward her. "I should call the police. Breaking and entering."

"The door was open. I heard about your head—" she gestured to his sore-looking scalp "—and when you didn't answer I got worried."

"I was working. I'm here for lunch and a little aloe."

She wanted to leave but her feet didn't move. "The puppies look good." That was a safe topic. She knew how to make small talk. She'd been taught the art by her mother and Grandmother Van Camp. Both women prided themselves on being able to start a conversation with anyone.

"I only have half an hour break. Was there anything else?"

"I guess not. Sorry about walking in." Her feet still didn't move. "I have sunscreen if you need it." She rummaged in her purse.

He stared at her. "Can't wear my hat," he finally said, turning toward his kitchen.

His stitches would make a hat uncomfortable. "What about a visor? Like you wear on a golf course?"

He snorted. "No." He dug in the refrigerator. He didn't tell her to go.

"Sit," she said. "I'll make you something. Least I can do for breaking into your place and for you taking such good care of Mama. Why don't you go slather yourself with aloe. You might want to get a bandanna to cover your—" She gestured to his red scalp.

"Her name's Maggie May," he said and left.

"Maggie May? Like that woman in that song. She was an older woman, too." She wouldn't think too hard on what that might or might not mean. Talking to the dog, Clover said, "I would never have believed it, but Danny Leigh can actually look ugly." She found fixings for a sandwich and soup in the fridge. She poured him a glass of iced tea and told herself she'd leave as soon as he got back from the bathroom…and she had a chance to visit with the puppies. Could she take one for herself? How would that work in a New York apartment and with her crazy hours? When her father finally named her CFO, her life would never be the same. She'd happily put in the twelve-hour days, the weekends and holidays. She really wanted to sink her teeth into the numbers.

While Danny was still doing whatever, Clover strolled to the pile of puppies. The fluffy white baby dog gnawed on her finger as the others fought over positions for the best milk.

"You'd better get back in there or you'll be hungry," she said softly as she nudged the puppy toward its mother.

"Hulk is the littlest. His brothers and sister push him out of the way," Danny said from behind her.

"He's very cute. I'm sure he'll be the first to be adopted." She turned around to tell Danny his lunch was ready and burst out laughing. His face and head were covered in green aloe vera gel. He looked like a swamp monster who'd been in the sun too long.

In addition to his scalp and nose, Danny's cheeks reddened. "I don't have any of the clear stuff."

She really did try to not laugh. "Now I know why they sell the clear stuff. You're sporting a facial-gone-wrong vibe now." She laughed again as a blob of the gel fell to his shirt and he frowned.

"Great. I'm going to have to change." He stomped off.

A well-timed retreat was called for. "I'm going, Danny. Food's on the table and let me know about the puppies."

"Wait," he yelled from his bedroom, which was just a few feet from the kitchen. Actually, everything in the apartment was just a few feet away.

He came back pulling on a T-shirt, his body revealed from his taut abs to his well-muscled chest and arms. That was certainly different from when they'd been young. He'd been teen-boy skinny. No more.

"The puppies and Maggie May will need to go to the vet. I can't take time away from my projects. Would you be able to take them?"

"Absolutely. Just let me know when. My schedule is fairly flexible."

"Other than when you're outbidding legitimate businessmen."

"My offer was legitimate and so is VCW's proposal."

"The town council will decide that," he said. Looking down at her, his gaze was stern and stubborn.

"You're right. I want the same thing for Angel Crossing as you do. It's just that VCW and I are going about it from a different avenue."

"More like a major highway."

There was no use going over the argument. "The food is on the table. You said you didn't have a lot of time."

"Crap. Maggie May needs to go out."

"I already did that. She did her business and everything."

"Thanks," he said, and it sounded like he meant it. Why did that little word start a glow in her? This stubborn cowboy—who currently looked like an extra in a horror film—could make her hot one second and mad as anything the next.

"Happy to help. Let me know about the appointment." She fled the apartment, not liking that she no longer wanted to laugh or hit him. Instead, she wanted to kiss him. The spark between them was still there.

Clover might have learned early on how to put on a good face for the world, but she'd also learned over the years how to be completely honest with herself. The honest-to-God truth was that she had the hots for Danforth Clayton Leigh. Wasn't that just a kick in the head?

Chapter Seven

Of course Clover was at Jim's. Danny just wanted to sit on a bar stool, enjoy his brew and stumble home. But, no, Miss Steer Princess had to be in his bar. To be fair, there was only one bar in Angel Crossing, but she could have gone to Tucson. In fact, she was the kind of woman who looked like she'd never stepped foot outside of a big city.

He ordered his beer and glared at Clover and Pepper. They were probably plotting the downfall of every man in town.

"What's got you in a mood, Mayor?" asked Rita, Anita's twin sister. "That woman here to buy up the whole town? Would think you'd like that, seeing as how you own properties that she just might want to buy."

"Maybe I'm not selling. I've got plans."

"Yep?"

He took a gulp of beer. "She wants to change everything. She and her father and Van Camp Worldwide. What kind of name is that?"

Rita shrugged. "Heard council might say yes to her proposition."

"They're still deciding. Irvin and Loretta are fighting about it. It might mean a lot of people will end up being bought out or pushed out. I read through what was submitted by Clo...Van Camp Worldwide. The community gardens will go, which is why I can't imagine why Pepper is over there talking with her."

"Keep your enemies closer," Rita said cryptically.

He'd like to get close with this particular enemy. Although he was pretty sure that was his lackluster love life talking. Look at his friend Darren. He'd gotten married two years ago, just as Danny "retired," and now his first baby was on the way. The numbness in Danny's hand and arm had been why he'd quit, but could it be he left bull riding for another reason, like one having to do with settling down?

Except he was spending all of his time and money buying properties and fixing them up for other people. Exactly how was any of that getting him closer to being a family man? The pressure from his mom had even eased now that she had a grandbaby. He was sure Lavonda would soon announce that she and Jones, her Scotsman, were expecting. Lavonda had even told him Clover's plan might be good for her fledgling trail and guide business, appealing to people looking for the treasure that her archaeologist husband insisted was still out there.

He signaled for a refill. He had thinking to do. He couldn't believe he hadn't been accosted by a resident. Usually when he was out, people stopped by to say hi, complain or pass along tidbits of gossip.

"Looks like that lady is stealing your thunder," Rita said as she gave him the refilled mug.

He shrugged.

"Are the two of you an item?"

"When we were teenagers."

"Heard you were canoodling on her porch."

"I wouldn't call it canoodling." What the hell did that even mean?

Rita pushed at her 1970s bleached blond hair. "Necking, then? Swapping spit? Playing tonsil hockey?"

He hoped the bar's dimness hid his blush. He tried a nonchalant shrug.

"She'd have to have a lot of intestinal fortitude to neck with you now. No offense, Mayor, but you're missing a tooth, half of your hair is gone and your face is peeling like a molting snake."

Danny wasn't vain. At least he hadn't thought he was until he'd looked in the mirror the last two mornings. "All temporary."

Rita nodded. "She looks high maintenance. Check out the purse and those boots. Still, she does drink beer and even ate deep-fried jalapeños."

"Her mama's a Texan. Daddy's from New York City."

"Really? Now, that's interesting." Rita turned from Danny. "Hold on. I'm coming," she said to someone over her shoulder. "You were too pretty before. You're finally starting to look like a real man. Clover seems like a woman who can appreciate that."

Clover's auburn hair tumbled down her back in big snaky curls and he could imagine the curve of her hips and breasts, just what a man would want next to him in bed. Soft enough for comfort, but strong, too. Clover turned suddenly, like she'd read his thoughts, and smiled with a devilish curl that heated him up. Pepper turned to see where Clover was looking. Damn. Pepper waved him over.

"Hey," he said to Pepper. "Clover." He tipped his head, missing his hat, which was still too heavy to rest on the stitches.

"We were just talking about you," Pepper said with a gleam.

"You were?"

"I explained to Clover how you helped me and AJ and that you worked miracles with those state agencies. I think you're wasting your talent here in Angel Crossing. You could run for state office. Maybe not now, but when you get your tooth fixed and your hair grows back."

"I like Angel Crossing," he said automatically.

"I know you do," Pepper said, "but you're still young. You don't want to be stuck here."

"You're no older than I am." He tried to not notice how well Clover's shirt fit. "I think going back to bull riding would be better for me than politics."

Pepper laughed. Clover looked both surprised and like she cared.

"I'd say the majority of people coming to SAC are coming to see you ride," Pepper said. "I bet if you ran for office, you'd win because everyone would remember your name and your bull riding."

"Is that why you're opposing my plan? Because it'll look good when you run for office?" Clover asked.

Was she serious? "I told you that I was a write-in for mayor and only won after a card draw. I don't have any political ambitions."

"Whether you do or not," Pepper said, "you should think about it. You could make a difference. Now that

Clover has company, I'm heading home before my daughter and husband think I've gotten lost."

Neither he nor Clover had a chance to stop her. Danny stood for a moment, not sure what he should do. He sat. Clover took a sip of beer. "You want another one?" he asked.

"Not yet," she said, giving him a look he couldn't read. "Why wouldn't you want to run for state office?"

"Because I have a business here and a commitment. I take both of those seriously." Now, of course, he might not have much of a business if Van Camp Worldwide got its way. Under Clover's plan, his properties couldn't be converted into homes or even apartments. Even if he got out of his project, he doubted he could go back on the road with bull riding. He couldn't do what he'd done for years with an arm and hand that weren't 100 percent.

"So why did you retire from bull riding? You still haven't told me."

And I won't, he thought to himself, although it would be easy to tell Clover the whole story. He'd always been able to talk to her. "It was time."

"That's what you said to the reporters. But what was the real reason? Your sister Lavonda is a PR genius. I bet she told you to say that."

"I didn't talk to Lavonda or anyone in the family about it." He took a long drink. "I'm getting another. You sure I can't get you a refill?" She shook her head.

He was supposed to be here to forget everything, not to examine his life choices. He pushed his mug forward for Rita. Why was he beginning to feel like he was at another crossroads, like the night he'd flipped the card and become mayor? He shook his head. He was getting as fanciful as Pepper's mother, Faye, who believed in astrological signs and energy vortices.

Rita started to draw his draft and talked over her shoulder to him. "I see you're getting reacquainted. You two look real good together, you know."

"That so. She's a good-looking woman."

"More than that," Rita said. "She's got more than cotton candy between her ears."

"She's got an MBA." That little fact still stunned him. The Clover he'd known had been all about the clothes and the hair.

Rita set down his mug but didn't let it go. "You're not the kind of cowboy who should be alone."

"Not much choice in Angel Crossing."

"Seems like you've got a good chance right there." She nodded to the table. "She watched you walk up here. You know women like to look, too. Why she'd want you now, who knows?" Rita pushed the beer at him.

Should he be taking dating advice from the woman who served him drinks? Why the hell not? Ending his dry spell with an old lover just made sense now that he thought about it. He might not be the smartest cowboy, but even he knew that she'd enjoyed kissing him. She'd not be staying in Angel Crossing for very long. That would mean no chance of a messy breakup where he had to see her every day like he would with anyone else in town. He smiled without showing off his missing tooth. Dang. Why couldn't he have come to this decision before his disasters or a week from now when they'd all be healed or replaced?

"Danny, I know you just got a drink," Clover said

as he sat down and took his first sip, "but let's go back to my place."

He dropped the mug to the table, splashing himself with beer. "Damn it."

CLOVER SWALLOWED HER laughter and nervousness. It wasn't that she was a shy, retiring wallflower. She was a grown woman who'd traveled the world and was the next in line to run her father's business. She'd decided that she wanted closure on her relationship with Danny. For her, that meant sleeping with him again and proving she was good at it. She might have been older than Danny when they'd first hooked up, but he'd had a lot of make-out experience.

Danny looked down at his wet crotch. She laughed. He gave her the half smile that had always gotten her hot and bothered. "Go back to your house to talk about Angel Crossing?" he asked.

"Maybe." The longer he took to leave with her, the more nerve she lost. If they didn't leave in the next five minutes, she'd totally chicken out.

"What else could be between us?" he asked, his gaze steady on hers.

She stood and moved closer so the entire bar wouldn't hear her. There'd be enough talk when they left together. "Bad sex."

"Bad?"

"Really bad. The worst. Is that how you want me to remember you?" She'd play to his ego, not that her own didn't need stroking. She smiled at her double entendre. She must really be losing it if that amused her.

"I have learned a lot since then," he said softly, leaning into her so his lips just brushed her ear. "And

I'm still the Boy Scout and I always make sure I'm 'prepared.'"

She shivered. *Oh, my.* "Me, too," she said, turning her head to brush her lips along the cords of his neck, where she could feel the quiver that raced through him. Good to know she wasn't the only one who was affected. She was doing this. She would prove to him she'd grown up and was a woman through and through. More important, she'd prove to herself that she could get over this old flame. "So, what are we waiting for?"

His blue gaze stayed locked on hers, searching. Then he smiled, covering his missing tooth but still looking sexy, dangerous and strangely familiar. "Ladies first— as it always should be."

"Can't argue with that, can I?" she asked softly, starting out of the bar, knowing that Danny would follow her. She turned off the numbers part of her brain, the part that would tell her being with Danny might be a mistake. This wasn't about her brain. This was about getting emotional closure.

The night was cool at this elevation, even if the days were warm. Danny wrapped his arm around her and she snuggled into his warmth, drinking in the comfort of his nearness. An awful lot for one hug.

"You haven't seen any ghosts?" he asked as they walked along the quiet streets.

"Not even an odd noise."

"Disappointed?"

"A little. Who wouldn't want to see at least one ghost in her life?"

"I almost thought that's what you were when I saw you again."

"Not very flattering." She wasn't sure where this was going or how it was making her feel.

"I'd been thinking about that summer recently, and then there you were. Maybe *surreal* is the better word."

"What about now? What does this feel like?"

"This," he said into her hair as she felt his light kiss, "is where I need to be."

"I agree. Come on—let's get moving." She rolled out of his hug, took his hand and tugged him toward her house. No more thinking, no more worrying.

She pulled him inside, closed the door and pushed him up against it so she could kiss him with everything that had been pent up inside her. She slipped her tongue into his mouth. He opened to her, allowing her to explore before he delved into her mouth. Then his hands cupped her buttocks, pulling her up against him. She dug her fingers into his shoulders to hold herself steady and to make sure that he stayed right where he was. They fit together even better than she remembered. She started to melt. She wanted him, but she also wanted this to last, wanted to drag out the pleasure to make sure he wouldn't forget her and walk away.

She paused. This was supposed to be about closure, not convincing him to stick around. She kissed him long and deep, forcing herself not to think, losing herself in the pleasure of his calloused fingers caressing her sides and slipping into the top of her jeans.

"This way," she finally said. They would be doing more than necking, and they weren't going to do it against the front door. She made it three steps before he pulled her back to him, snuggling her butt into his crotch and wrapping her in his arms so he could gently cup her breasts. Her head fell back onto his shoulder with pleasure. He took advantage of her vulnerable neck, nibbling at the sensitive skin. From the tips of her breasts to the place just behind her ear, Clover had become one exposed nerve ending. She wrenched away to lead him to the bedroom. She wanted him, but in her own way. He followed, taking time to stroke her shoulder, his breath coming in deep gusts.

The bedroom was tiny with just a double bed. She hadn't had much choice and hadn't planned to share it. At least it would mean getting close. "Come here," she said. "I want to undress you."

"Undress me?" Danny asked, his hands loose at his sides. The rest of his body was as a taut as a bow.

She didn't say more, but approached him and started with the snaps on his shirt, opening one, kissing him and then putting her hands under the fabric to feel every inch of his skin. She stopped on the ridge of a scar.

He turned his darkened gaze on her. "Few stitches when I got pinned while moving cattle for a friend." She nodded. Another button, more skin. Warm with the tough muscle underneath that made her feel at once protected and on edge. He was so strong. She had to give him her complete trust. This man who was nearly a stranger, except he wasn't.

"I would never hurt you," he said, reading her thoughts through her skin.

She shivered for a moment, but shook her head. "You still have on too many clothes." She tugged at his jeans. He stopped her, his hand grappling for his wallet. She knew what he wanted and didn't let him search for the protection. With a knowing grin, she pulled out the condom, tossed the wallet and shimmied down his underwear. He sprang free, proving he was more than interested in what she'd started. She pushed against him until he lay on the bed.

"You," he rasped. "Your clothes."

She took off her shirt.

"The bra," he said. "Undo it slowly."

She complied, trying to think about the sexy striptease she'd seen in movies, except things didn't go exactly as planned when she couldn't get the hooks to unhook. Danny helped, placing a kiss on her shoulder.

"Out of those jeans, princess," he commanded.

She stood so he could watch and slowly peeled out of her pants. She stood naked, vulnerable and not feeling as powerful as she'd hoped. He sat up and reached out his hands to grab her hips and pull her toward him, placing a kiss on her belly, making her shiver with delight.

When she was on the bed with him, he took the condom from her and…they were going to do this. He entered her and she raised herself to him. Their hips slapped together in an out-of-sync rhythm. Then she leaned forward, moved and their foreheads knocked. Oh, no, not again. It was like the first time—awkward, uncoordinated and unsatisfying.

Danny held himself still until Clover relaxed. "Princess," he whispered in her ear as he pulled her onto her side with him. So they could face each other. So they were equals. "I want to be with you more than I've ever wanted anything. But I want us to both want this. Tell me what to do."

"Kiss me," Clover said. So he did, softly tasting her lips while his fingers skimmed her back. She heated and softened again. He moved. She moaned into his mouth.

"Better?" he asked.

Clover used her legs to pull him close, his body and hands loving her. She didn't want it to end and was afraid she couldn't take more.

"Clover, I'm going to take you to the moon and back." And he did.

Chapter Eight

Danny stood over Clover, watching her sleep. The moonlight from the window highlighted the creamy perfection of her skin. Her lips were red and puffy. They'd proved more than once they were no longer awkward teens. He hoped this one night would be enough. But what if it wasn't?

He'd faced his fears more than once; he could do it again. First, he needed to get out of Dead Man's Cottage. There were the puppies and Maggie May to care for and his apartment was probably a mess. He looked down at Clover again. One last time. He leaned forward, but, no, not one more kiss. She mumbled in her sleep and turned under the sheets. He held his breath. She snuggled into the pillow. Turning away, he slipped out of the house, stopping his shout when he stubbed his toe hard on the front porch chair. He sat on the steps to pull his boot on over his now aching foot. What was it about Clover being back in his life and his quotient of accidents hitting an all-time high? At this rate, he'd collect more injuries than he had in all the time he'd been a bull rider.

The streets of Angel Crossing were quiet and dark as he made his way across town. He heard Maggie

May whining from his landing and hurried to open the door. She rushed past to take care of business. He checked on the puppies. All fine. Moments later Maggie May came up for a pet before climbing back in with her babies. He went to bed, but he couldn't sleep.

Clover wasn't for him. She wanted to ruin his town by turning it into a place where people like her and her family would be comfortable. And where people like him and the rest of the town would be the employees. Angel Crossing was a workingman's town—Ford pickups, Wrangler jeans and Spam. He'd read in her proposal that there would be Michelin restaurants and spas behind the wooden facades. That would just take the heart out of the town. Lem's general store and Jim's would be gone. Maybe not right away but how could they compete? Those kinds of businesses, along with the people who patronized them, were what made Angel Crossing Angel Crossing. Take that away and what did you have? Some cardboard town.

He shouldn't have been surprised by the type of plan she'd presented. Clover had been a princess in more ways than one. He always figured she'd gone after him because he wasn't from her world and would upset her parents. He wondered if, years later, things were much different. Maybe not, but he wasn't the same. He needed to worry about Angel Crossing.

He turned onto his side, closing his eyes and telling himself to go to sleep. He had a job tomorrow, and he needed to talk to and convince another property owner that Danny's plan for the town was better than Clover's. He also needed to get back to training so he didn't disgrace himself at the charity bull-riding extravaganza. His life was too full to worry about what he may or may not want to do with Clover, Miss Steer Princess.

DANNY'S LEG JITTERED as he waited for the council to get to the only item on the agenda that mattered: Van Camp Worldwide's requests…blah, blah, blah. The legalese Bobby Ames had used couldn't hide the fact that the company's—Clover's—request would change his town. Instead of using his powers of persuasion to talk business, he'd gone to bed with Clover. Stupid. Stupid. Stupid. A week and a half later, more and more Angelites seemed to be on her side.

Bobby said in his best *Law & Order* voice, "We will now consider Van Camp Worldwide's Rico Pueblo proposal. Is there a representative from the company here?"

Of course there was. She was sitting in the front row, looking like a cross between a Texas beauty queen and a corporate tight ass. How did she do that and look sexy on top of all of it? Her lush lips…the bright color of her clothes making her skin look like silk and her hair like a flame. Dear Lord.

Clover stood. "Thank you, Mr. President."

"Call me Bobby."

She smiled and Danny refused to be jealous. Bobby was old enough to be her daddy.

"Bobby, then," Clover said. "I've spoken with all of you as well as many members of the business community. Everyone has been very welcoming. They've understood the advantages of VCW's plan to transform your community and provide economic viability. For those looking for work and those looking to start or grow their businesses, I can see a range of possibilities."

"What about the cost of living?" Danny asked.

"Taxes will decrease with the influx of business. Plus, there will be opportunities for increased services for residents," she said, giving him a look that was all business.

"Hey, Bobby, I've got a question." Anita from Jim's spoke up. Her twin, Rita, sat next to her looking stern and unhappy. Good. At least two people were on his side. "What about those of us who already got a good business? I didn't see anything on your plan about that."

"If you look at page—"

"You're bringing in competition," said Lem, the owner of the general store.

"We'll also be bringing renewed interest in Angel Crossing," she said before being interrupted by a number of angry voices.

Finally Bobby cracked down his gavel. "That's enough. I will have order, and if I have to call the chief to arrest the disrupters, I will." The crowd quieted but not happily. Danny kept silent. It looked like he might have more support than he'd hoped.

Clover started again. "VCW is well aware of the worries and challenges of a project of this scope and importance. For that reason, even after we receive approval, we will continue to have open discussions with residents and property owners."

Loretta spoke up from her council seat. "I like you and your plan. Angel Crossing has been dying for years. Sure, we got that farmers' market, but that's not going to save us."

"She's right," Irvin, her husband, said, "and you offered our neighbor a fair price for his property."

Just like Danny had been able to read the shift of muscle that told him exactly how the bull he was sitting on would twist or turn, he felt the crowd starting to sway to a different direction. Dang. How had she done that and what could he say to get them back to opposing the plan?

"I also believe with these changes, your children and grandchildren will want to call Angel Crossing— Rico Pueblo—home," Clover said.

That was exactly what the older residents wanted to hear. They'd been complaining that their families were being split apart because there were no jobs or much of anything else for the young people.

"Wait," Danny said, but Anita talked over him.

"I saw that New York City snoot nose—" she pointed at Clover "—hit a dog with her car and not even stop." The audience gasped and glared in unison.

"I didn't—"

"I've seen the mayor caring for the dog and the puppies," Rita added.

"You hit a mama dog?" someone else in the audience said.

Danny felt the shift again, just like a bull ready to move from a right- to a left-footed spin. He could keep the bull on its current path or have it switch feet for a new turn. He'd guessed at the truth of the dog's injury and Clover's part in it, even though she hadn't fully confessed what had happened to him or anyone else, as far as he knew. He wanted to win this vote for the Angel Crossing he could imagine. If he won because he didn't stand up and explain the whole story, would he really have won? Hells yes. But he'd still feel guilty about it.

"Wait a minute," he said into the grumbling. "That's not exactly the way it happened."

"Are you calling me a liar?" Anita asked with a glare.

"No, ma'am." He gave her his sweetest smile, now back to normal since his tooth had been replaced. "It's just that you didn't have a chance to see what happened then or what Ms. Van Camp has done since the accident."

He couldn't decide if he saw relief, surprise or something warmer in Clover's bluebonnet eyes.

"Let the mayor speak," Bobby said.

"Miss Clover did hit the dog—" Danny started.

"See?" Rita and Anita said together.

"But—" Danny talked over them "—it was an accident. The dog came out of nowhere. That's happened to everyone at some time. A critter just ends up in your path." The bull was going into a spin and he'd hold on till the bell. "She stopped and tracked down the dog with my help. Then we took her out to Pepper, who patched her up. Miss Clover bought Maggie May a collar, food and everything else she needed. She's done what she could for her. She didn't mean to hit her. She might be here to change Angel Crossing, but she understands one thing about us. We look after our own and those less able to care for themselves. We help those who need it and don't ask for anything in return."

HELL, DAMNATION AND fire ants. How was she supposed to handle him being nice to her? Clover had been sure he'd let the bus driven by the twins from Jim's run her over. Instead, he'd defended her, even though he had been fighting hard against her plan. He didn't look at her now, keeping his gaze on the crowd. She couldn't say her presentation had gone well, but it hadn't gone badly either. She'd been trying everything she could think of to help the town understand what an opportunity VCW was offering them, their children and even their children's children.

"I think we've heard enough for tonight," Bobby said, looking at the audience and then at his fellow council members. "But I don't believe we're ready for a vote. I want to have our state representative go over your numbers, Miss Van Camp. There's also that section about options I'd like to review." The other council members bobbed their heads. She couldn't look at anyone because she didn't want them to see her disappointment and worry.

She smiled politely, as her Texas mama and grandmama had taught her. "I understand completely, but if you have any questions or concerns, I would love to address them now." Clover waited but no one said anything. She pressed on. "I understand the due diligence the council must have to ensure that Angel Crossing's interests are best met. However, I do want to point out that this plan is time sensitive and delaying a decision could negatively impact our project." She didn't need to let them know that it might also mean her father showing up. Something she didn't want. The entire reason she was here was to prove she could do the job better than her brother. Good enough to become the next CFO.

"We don't work on big-city time," said council member Marie Carmichael with a stern tone.

"I understand, ma'am," she answered. "Maybe the council could call a special meeting in two weeks for residents to ask questions before the decision is made?" That would help with the timing, although they were still cutting it close.

"That'll cost us for an advertisement and it isn't enough time," Bobby said. "Do I have a motion to table the proposal?" Before Clover could protest again, the plan was tabled and the meeting adjourned. Even as the council members left, she tried to convince them of the wisdom of calling a special meeting. Then she got pinned down in the hallway by the twins, who accused her of lying to the mayor about what had happened to the dog.

"Rita, Anita." Danny's voice came from behind her and she tried not to feel relieved. "I told you it was an accident that couldn't be avoided. She did the right thing by helping the animal. If you're so worried, how about you agree to take two of the puppies. One for each of you." Suddenly the fierce twins were back-pedaling and nearly ran out of the town hall.

"Thanks," Clover said.

"I might be many things, but I'm not a liar and I'm not going to let lies hurt someone else."

She nodded her head. "I guess I'll see you next month."

"Speaking of Maggie May and her offspring... would you like to see them? They've grown a lot since you saw them."

She hesitated, not sure that she wanted to be in his apartment and alone. No. She'd gotten closure. She didn't need closure a second time. "Absolutely. How long until they can be adopted?" she asked as they left the building.

"Good night, Mayor," one of the police officers said.

Danny gave him a wave of acknowledgment. For some reason, a flush of embarrassment heated her face. They weren't doing anything wrong.

"My sister's brother-in-law's sister-in-law is a vet tech and she said another three weeks and they'll be ready. The other problem is getting them to the vet in Tucson for their shots. I want to make sure that they're good to go for adoption."

"That's nice of you." There were times when Danny had surprised her with how thoughtful and caring he could be. He'd always had a particularly soft heart. She was glad to see that hadn't changed. Just glad in the abstract, though, not because she cared or expected the two of them to get any closer. Hadn't they already been as close as two people could get? That had just been closure. Nothing more.

"Jolene, the vet tech and my sister's…relative by marriage, should move here. I bet she could open a pet store or something and clean up. I wonder if she could open a clinic? I should check on that."

She didn't mention that soon Rico Pueblo would provide everything residents needed.

The walk to the apartment had been quick and almost furtive. Even so, they were noticed by more people than she would have imagined, each one taking time to say hello and make note of some problem or issue. Danny always smiled and answered politely but kept moving.

"You're good at that," she said as they climbed the steps to his apartment.

"At what?"

"Being mayor."

"You think so?"

"Absolutely. Consummate politician. You answered each person without promising anything."

He looked at her oddly before opening the door. "My landlord said I can keep the dogs for another six weeks. Then they've got to go."

"That gives you some time to get rid of them."

He flicked on the light and turned to her. "I'm not getting *rid* of them. I'll find good homes. They're not trash to throw away."

Wow. She'd hit a nerve. "I didn't choose my words well. I don't think they're trash."

Puppy yips and scrambling nails silenced them. Maggie May raced past them and out the door. The puppies struggled after her. "Catch them," Danny said as he moved to the furred horde. "We have to carry them down the stairs."

She picked up the little white puppy and another who looked like a cross between a shepherd and a beagle. She followed Danny into the back lot, putting down the little animals and laughing with him at their antics. Maggie May made sure they didn't wander too far. When all business was done, they carried the puppies back up the stairs with Maggie May at their heels.

In the apartment, Clover put down her two puppies in a corner that had been barricaded and lined with newspapers.

"They're getting better, but still have accidents if

I leave it too long between potty breaks," Danny explained. "Would you like a beer?"

What exactly did he mean by his invitation? Was he just being polite? He was a cowboy, after all, raised by a mama who expected a certain level of behavior. She'd learned that when they'd been a couple. Or did his invite mean something more? In either case, she was a big girl and could say yes or no as she pleased.

"Thanks. That would be nice." He smiled his patented Leigh smile of conquest. She nearly changed her mind. Then remembered that she was immune, inoculated by years of sophistication and a little kernel of hurt that remained from his rejection of her all of those years ago. Maybe the closure hadn't quite finished off that chapter.

"Here you go," he said, handing her a bottle and motioning for her to take a seat in the recliner as he pulled up a kitchen chair.

"I guess you don't have many visitors." He shook his head. "Do you have any leads on adopters?" Suddenly the room felt small, hot and full of promise. Had she really followed him out of her interest in the puppies? She looked over at the blocked-off area. When she turned back, Danny was right there beside her, looming over her. She shivered. Slowly he leaned down, pushing back the chair as his lips touched hers. She sighed in delight. He lay across her, holding himself up so that he didn't crush her but molded to her tightly enough that she felt every heated inch of him.

"I didn't come here for this," she gasped between his kisses.

"I didn't ask you here for this," he whispered across

her cheek. "But you are the sweetest, sexiest woman I've ever met, and I just can't resist tasting you."

And taste her he did, until they were both breathless, and then he took her to his bed. She urged him to go faster. He wouldn't listen, dragging out each touch, each brush of his lips, until she was begging him. When they did finally come together, she couldn't think, only feel.

She mumbled into his sweaty shoulder as she kissed him, "We can't keep meeting like this."

"Why not? Seems like the best nights I've spent in a Rocky Raccoon's age. Go to sleep before I'm tempted to show you again why we should keep meeting like this."

"Promises, promises, promises," she teased. And show her he did.

THE NEXT MORNING as Danny slept, she woke with Maggie May and the puppies, making her way down the stairs in one of Danny's oversize cowboy shirts. Of course, the white puppy, the runt yet the most adventuresome, hustled around the building. Clover yelled after him, fearful he would get to the street. She heard Danny coming down the steps, saying something to her as she went around the corner of the building.

"Hulk," she called.

"Clover?" her father asked, standing on the sidewalk looking at her with a frown.

"Clover," Danny called just as he came around the corner, "don't go out on the street without your—"

"Daddy," she said, interrupting Danny as she yanked at the shirt to magically make it longer. Maybe this was a nightmare.

Her father's frown deepened. "I sent you here to clean up your brother's mess and what are you doing but taking up with some drifter."

Chapter Nine

Danny's hand automatically went to his head to brush down his hair that had grown in but refused to lie down nicely. He stepped in front of Clover and stretched out his hand. "Good to see you, Heyer. I mean, Mr. Van Camp."

The tall man with a thick middle, hair plugs and a pinkie ring didn't take the hand.

"I'm Mayor Danny Leigh," he said, trying not to wince. Not exactly how he wanted to meet the man who had the fate of the town in his hands and was also Clover's daddy. He didn't need the man's approval, but no man wanted to meet a daddy half-dressed, making it clear what he'd just been doing with his daughter. "If you'd like to go on to the diner, we can meet you in a few minutes." Clover poked Danny hard in the back as she moved from behind him, holding the puppy like a shield.

"Daddy, where are you staying? I'll meet you there after I've had my shower and breakfast."

Danny saw the mean squint to the man's eyes and stepped in again. "If you give me two minutes, I can be ready to take you on a tour of the town. You can meet up with Miss Clover later."

"Don't try that 'yes, ma'am' cowboy bull crap on me. I remember you, boy," her daddy said in a blue-blood tone that made him feel about two inches high.

"I'm mayor of Angel Crossing and a lot of things have changed."

"Not everything," the older man said. "Clover, let's go. You can take me to where you're staying. We'll talk there without interference from the *mayor*."

Clover tried again. "I think it would be better for me to meet you later."

"Now, please," her father said in a voice used to command.

Danny couldn't believe the fierce take-no-prisoners Clover turned and hurried up the stairs. Danny wasn't sure whether to stay here and talk with her father or try to comfort Clover. He didn't know exactly what she needed to be comforted for but he knew that she needed it.

"So," the man said, rooting Danny to the spot, "you're after Clover again and you think being mayor makes you worthy of her now, do you?"

"Clover is a grown woman," Danny said. Because what else could he say?

"She may be but she has a lot of her mother in her. A little too much concern about love and not enough about facts. The fact is that Clover has the chance to—"

"I'm ready, Daddy," she said, hurrying up to them dressed in yesterday's suit and looking great despite the mussed hair, which he vividly remembered helping muss. "The paper in the puppy pen needs to be changed," she told Danny, dismissing him in a way he didn't like and didn't deserve.

He reached for her hand and, before she could stop him, pulled her close for a kiss, just to prove to her that he wasn't someone to be so easily forgotten. Dang. She tasted good and for a second she softened. Then she pushed—okay, shoved—him away.

"Mayor," she said in an icy tone. "We'll see you at the next meeting."

She walked off with her daddy. Danny stood watching and not doing a blasted thing.

To GET THE puppies used to life in Arizona, Danny took the wriggling animals and their mama for a ride in his pickup with strict orders (to the little ones) that there would be no piddling in the truck. The trip to see AJ had another purpose. Danny would show the pups to AJ's daughter, EllaJayne, who would see the animals and instantly fall in love. It might be a dirty trick but he needed to find good homes for the puppies. AJ's ranch was a perfect place. Could Danny convince him that two were better than one?

"All right, boys and girl," he said to the box of puppies. "It's showtime. Be on your cutest behavior."

Butch, AJ's girlfriend's dog, came running up to him with his friendly tail wagging furiously. Danny looked around for AJ, figuring he wouldn't be far behind. The llamas and alpacas were milling in the corral and the fields of vegetables stretched out in every direction. Here was one of the people Danny wanted to protect by fighting Clover and her daddy's company. It wasn't just his own plans. Others had invested in Angel Crossing, too, including his own sister, who had a tour-guide business. She'd been in PR with big corporations. She understood how all of this worked, so maybe she could help him. On the other hand, he hated running to his big sister for help like a little boy.

Danny heard a yip, a growl and pounding hooves. Dang it. The puppies had escaped. He'd forgotten they were actually mobile now. They had, of course, found their way into the corral with the furballs, as AJ called the alpacas, llamas…and goats? When had he gotten goats? Hairy goats with big horns. Butch and Maggie May ran past Danny and toward the corral. That unfroze Danny and he sprinted for the animals. Crap. Clover would kill him if the animals got hurt.

Butch had one puppy in his mouth and Maggie May another, the two of them coming out of the corral as Danny climbed in. The big animals seemed to be stepping delicately around the racing puppies. Danny caught another quickly and deposited him back outside the corral with Butch. The dog guarded the two puppies. Good. Danny went back in for the last one—Hulk. He might be the runt, but he had the most personality, 100 percent fearsome. Today that meant he was having a growl-off with a large billy goat, who had been tolerating the nonsense. Now he lowered his head, ready to butt the puppy into kingdom come.

Danny hurried forward to scoop up Hulk, who readied himself to leap at the goat. He got the pup into his arms, stumbled forward, just as the goat rammed, hitting Danny solidly in the nose. He fell to the ground and saw stars, moons and rainbows.

"Hey, Norman, get away from him," a woman's voice said, followed by AJ's loud whistle. Danny breathed in carefully, trying to figure out what might or might not be broken. Hulk licked his cheeks.

"Danny?" Pepper asked. He felt more than heard

her kneel, and then her fingers were checking him over in a professional manner.

"I'm okay," he managed to say around the pain in the middle of his face. Damn it. Had the goat broken his nose?

"I don't think you're okay. Stay right where you are. AJ, come and get this puppy and give him back to his mama and lock them up in the barn. Don't let EllaJayne see any of them." During all of that, Pepper didn't stop her examination, moving his head and neck. He winced and the movement made his nose shift into a new level of throbbing pain. "I know I took an oath and all, but I'm almost ready to let you lie out here. Bringing puppies—that's low."

"Just taking them for a ride."

"Uh-huh. Right now, though, I'm going to be the bigger person and treat you. You didn't break your nose, but the bruising will sure feel like it. You also strained muscles in your neck. As soon as AJ gets back, we'll help you into the house. I need to get ice on the nose and pack it. You're bleeding everywhere."

"I am?" he asked but it sounded more like "niam nam?"

"You are." She swatted away the hand he'd lifted to feel his nose and wipe away the blood.

Without fuss, AJ and Pepper got him into the Santa Faye Ranch's original homestead. Their own new home wasn't completed...yet. The residents of Angel Crossing were helping them get the house up as fast as possible, but money and time were both in short supply. He sat in the kitchen chair as Pepper, a physician's assistant, worked on him, helped by her mother, who believed fervently in the power of astrology and

Summer of Love medicine she'd learned from who knew where. He winced as Pepper found a particularly sore spot in his neck and swallowed a moan when the movement made his packed and iced nose throb.

"Definitely a strain. Faye, get me the aspirin."

"I think he'd do better with willow bark and turmeric."

Through his nearly closed eyes, he saw Pepper get the painkillers. He hoped it would help. His head had started to pound now, too.

"Here," she said, handing him a glass. He reached out with his right hand without thinking and the glass slipped from it. Dang it. "That's it. You're going to the hospital. Faye, call 911."

"No," Danny said, sitting straight up despite the surge of pain. "I'm okay."

"You've done something more to your neck than strain the muscles. Sit still. You don't want to make it worse."

"It's not new," he managed to mumble out. At least that was what he hoped she heard.

"Not new. What have you done to yourself and why haven't you seen me?"

He'd have to confess now. AJ stood in the doorway with his daughter, EllaJayne. Great. Why not just announce it in the paper? But from the determined look on Pepper's face, he had little choice. He worked on speaking as clearly as his aching and stuffed nose would allow. "I have…numbness in my right hand and arm. Doctors said it might be something with my back or with the joints. Told me it might get better with rest."

"Obviously that hasn't happened," Pepper said sternly.

"It's better some days than others. But I've been doing a bit of practice for SAC. It's acting up again."

"You need to have it checked," Pepper said.

AJ stepped forward and laid his hand on her shoulder. "Let him be. He's a bull rider. He knows what he's about."

"Trying to cause permanent damage to himself."

"One little ride won't do that," AJ said. "I thought there was a bit more to the story of you retiring."

Danny nodded. Becoming mayor had happened just as he needed to make a decision about riding.

Pepper stepped away from AJ. "I don't care about your bull-rider code or whatever it is. You can't ride with that numbness."

"I'm teaching myself to use my other hand. It's not a real competition, just for fun."

"Puppies," EllaJayne screamed. Every adult eye turned. A proud Butch sat surrounded by four puppies posed in exactly the same way.

"Oh, my," Faye said. "I didn't know it was the Year of the Dog."

CLOVER REALLY WANTED a drink, but since Rita and Anita at Jim's were dead set against her father, VCW and Rico Pueblo, she'd have to go to the Devil's Food Diner for coffee and pie. Her head might appreciate it in the morning, but her thighs would be hating it when she upped her workout. She'd start by walking to the diner from her house. It would give her time to try to figure out what her father was up to besides proving that she'd made a mess of things. He'd been ignoring her and had even set up a meeting with the council president that she hadn't been invited to.

She sped up her walk to outpace the voice that whispered to her that her father would never respect her and never believe that she could handle anything without him checking on every detail. She made it to the diner in record time.

Danny's sister Lavonda called to her, "Are you by yourself? Come sit with us."

Danny was the reason she was at the diner ready to drown her sorrows in lemon meringue pie. *That* morning two weeks ago was the real reason she and her father had been fighting about everything. Finding her wearing only Danny's shirt had been really, really bad luck. She blushed remembering it.

"Come on," Lavonda urged. "You've got to see the cutest baby in the universe."

Clover walked over, intrigued because she knew the baby wasn't Lavonda's. She had a donkey and a cat and a Scotsman but no baby.

She looked for Jessie, Danny's oldest sister and the baby's mama. There she was, striding from the hallway that led to the bathrooms. "Thanks for watching Gertie," said Jessie when she got to the table. "Hey, Clover, heard you were still in town."

Clover wondered if this was a setup. The women had been very protective of their little brother even as teens. Could she gracefully leave? No, she could not. She sat down and admired the baby with Jessie's smile and, disconcertingly, Danny's blue eyes. Her dark hair was apparently from her surgeon father.

After pie and coffee had been ordered and the baby

resettled into her car seat for a nap, the two Leigh girls turned on Clover—as she'd guessed they would.

Lavonda started. "You know I spent years in corporate communications. I'd like to know exactly how you can promise you won't be pushing out current business owners and residents who don't sell."

"I've outlined that in the presentation. We don't control economics, but those businesses that take advantage of the influx of visitors will certainly have the opportunity to thrive. Take your guide business, Lavonda. More people coming to Rico Pueblo must include those interested in exploring the desert or looking for the Scottish treasure, right? We project that within five years the average stay will be two weeks."

"Isn't there a housing component?" Lavonda asked.

"A part of the plan is for condo-style housing that will be managed by VCW. It will allow people to make this their second home or a vacation retreat."

"What about Danny?" Jessie asked, her sage-green eyes fierce. "He wants to help families here afford housing. It sounds like your plans will push them out. There's Pepper, too, and her market."

This was tricky because the approval of Rico Pueblo would be the end to Danny's plans. The properties he'd bought would remain zoned as commercial. "He could shift his project farther from the core of the town, possibly."

Lavonda said firmly, "The point, though, was that the residents could walk to what they needed—the doctor, the market and Lem's store. Moving them farther from town will mean they need to drive, which some don't do or shouldn't do. Having an affordable core was also attractive to younger home buyers. This town definitely needs younger folks and a place for the children of the current Angelites to start off."

"Two things. With the influx of tourists, there could be a public transit system. Second, VCW and Rico Pueblo will provide jobs that will help keep younger people here. There'll be viable career opportunities."

"Huh." Jessie snorted. "I don't see the people here wanting to ride those cute little trolleys like they have in Tucson and Phoenix. And careers? Sweeping up at restaurants and washing dishes?"

Clover wasn't going to argue about the clear economic pluses of the plan. Instead, she said, "It's not up to me, really. The council will make the final decision on whether our project is best for the town. I think that makes it fair all around."

"It would be," Jessie said, "if Danny had your money for slick presentations and throwing around the promise of good prices for land. A couple of property owners told me that you...sorry, your father and VCW... offered them above-market prices for their properties."

Clover scrambled to understand why her father was making offers. She was supposed to be doing that, as they'd decided in New York months ago.

"Plus, you're sleeping with our brother," Jessie said. Her stubborn cowgirl chin thrust out. "What are you trying to do? Convince him of your way of thinking with—"

"Of course not!" She was hurt to her core that these women would think she'd do something like that.

"Good," Lavonda said. "At least you're not using Danny's 'interest' in you to get your own way. We wondered about that."

"I'll be leaving," Clover said with as much Texas

beauty queen as she could manage. "Everything I'm doing in Angel Crossing is legal and ethical. I resent that you would imply anything else."

Clover walked out of the diner quickly, not even paying for her pie and coffee. After the grilling, the Leigh sisters could take care of that. Half a block down the sidewalk, Clover had cooled off enough to get back to the biggest surprise in the conversation. Why was her father buying properties and paying above-market price? She needed to confront him about his interference. She was an adult woman and could certainly stand up to her daddy. As long as he didn't bring up Danny and that morning. No. She could face that, too, and hold her head high.

Chapter Ten

Danny stood watching with nothing like excitement as AJ helped his former boss unload the bull. They were setting up a little practice ride at the small out-door stadium near the community college, where the charity bull-riding extravaganza would take place in just over two months.

The bull his friend had found for him had enough pep to give Danny a workout without the full force of the spins and bucks of a competition ride. It would give him a chance to practice riding with his left hand. Right now, the numbness in his right was barely there, but it could be full-on numb at any time, something that would be dangerous if it happened during a ride. If his hand was numb, how could he grip the bull rope? It would be a good chance to get hurt really bad.

"DD here is a good bull," AJ said as they got everything ready in the chute. Danny's guts churned. It felt like a really, really long time since he'd climbed aboard a bull. What the hell had he been thinking? "He'll give you a good ride without thinking he needs to kill you."

"You're the expert." Danny gritted his teeth as he prepped himself. It all felt so wrong. The wrong hand, the wrong bull, the wrong arena. Except he'd promised his town he'd do this. He'd also promised himself that he hadn't quit riding because he had to. He'd prided himself that he'd known when to get out. This event would prove to himself that he could've kept riding if he'd wanted to.

"Dave will be out there to help you off, if you need it. But this old bull is easy. No worries. Dave uses him a lot for his classes and clinics. He knows the drill."

Crap. It sounded like AJ thought he was a rookie. "You know how many buckles I have?"

"Yep. And I also know you haven't ridden for at least two years, and you're using your left hand."

"Always said I could ride with one hand tied behind my back."

"That one of your mama's sayings?"

Anger flared through Danny, making him want to punch his longtime friend. He pulled in a breath to calm himself. He couldn't ride like that. He needed a certain amount of quiet in his brain to ready himself for the ride. He worked to find that place where everything went quiet, calm. He nodded his head that he was ready, but instantly the calm was gone and it was too late to change his mind. AJ had released DD and the bull knew his business. He bolted from the chute and lifted his hindquarters in a mighty buck. Danny stayed centered…barely. He worked to find the rhythm of the animal's stride and buck. It just wasn't there. He could feel the animal bunching its body for a spin, cursed and went flying. The dirt of the arena hadn't gotten any softer. DD stood quietly, tail flicking. He really was a beginner's animal. Crap.

Danny stood and dusted himself off. AJ was looking at him oddly, maybe a little worried. Danny waved his hat and went back to the chute. He would have a bruise on his hip, but otherwise he was good. He'd climb back on board after giving the bull a rest. This was just practice. You fell when you practiced so you didn't when it came time for the big show.

"ONE MORE TIME," he told AJ after another three-second ride.

"Not sure DD wants to."

"He's barely gotten a workout."

"Dave," AJ yelled. "One more?"

The stockman considered the request, then nodded. The bull had let him test his left arm. Though the animal was barely working to unseat him, Danny couldn't figure out exactly why he was having such trouble. Staying on the bull should have been easy. This time he'd do it. He'd clear his mind properly and get his seat settled. Number four was the charm, right?

He could've sworn as he settled himself on DD again the bull gave him the side eye. *You again, fool?* Danny silently told the bull to shut it. He was a two-time champion with multiple picture-perfect rides and more buckles than days of the week. He would ride this old bull and win this time. He nodded to AJ, and in that split second Clover's face popped into his mind. He ate dirt. Damn it.

"What the hell, cowboy?" AJ said.

DD didn't even have the momentum to keep going. He stood by Danny and AJ snorting…laughing before trotting toward Dave, who was holding out the bull's favorite treat: marshmallows.

"Bee flew at me," Danny lied. He wouldn't tell AJ

that Clover had distracted him. He'd always said no matter how many women he chased, they'd never come between him and a bull. "I'll do more conditioning. I know what I've got to work on now."

"Like how to ride a bull? You were better your rookie year. What's wrong?" The last was asked with the serious tone of a good friend with worries.

"Been longer than I thought since I climbed aboard. I'll be ready to try again as soon as you can line something up."

"If you say so. Let me help Dave. Then I'll buy you a beer."

"Sorry. I've got to go. Mayor stuff," Danny lied. He didn't want to talk to AJ about his failure and what was at the root of it. He wanted to go home, shower and brood. The best he could do was brood on the drive home because there was a handyman job he'd been promising to finish up and another small project he needed to bid on. Both could probably be put off until tomorrow, but right now he wanted to keep busy.

On the way to the job, he analyzed the rides, as his late friend Gene had taught him and AJ to do. He hadn't been able to get the right rhythm or feel of the bull using his left hand. He couldn't believe that it made such a difference. He couldn't believe he'd never had to ride that way because of a broken bone or a strain. Or maybe being teenager-stupid had made it easier. Next practice, he'd have to use his right hand and hope that it didn't decide to go numb at the wrong time.

AJ AND HIS former boss Dave showed up with another practice bull a few days later. This one was DD's son, fierier than his father but still a good practice animal.

He wasn't fond of turning corkscrews or more challenging bucks, making him not-so-popular with the professionals but perfect for training.

Today Danny had prepared himself to use his less reliable right hand in the hope he could find his rhythm again. Waiting for AJ and Dave to get Black Fury into the chute, Danny pictured what he would do for each twist and turn of the bull. He then cleared his mind, focusing on a tuft of hair on the bull's head as he lowered himself on the animal, who twitched at the weight but otherwise didn't move. Danny found his seat and the calm he'd been looking for last time. He nodded and the gate opened. The bull crow-hopped, then threw up its back legs. Danny easily rode out those maneuvers until he heard AJ yell "Eight," and he easily jumped from the bull.

Dave corralled the animal and Danny knew he had his mojo back. He'd be able to ride in the event and not make a fool of himself. It felt right, too. The smell of dust and heated animal. The creak of the leather under him. All of it added up to a weirdly comfortable place.

"Well, hell," AJ said as Danny went back to the chute. "Look who showed up to watch."

Danny squinted into the stands and saw the sun glinting off auburn. Damn. Clover was here. Why was Clover here? He wanted to be 110 percent on his game before anyone saw him riding. He was at 85 or so. Another three weeks of conditioning and practice rides would get him there with plenty of time left over before the event. He wanted to do all of that without an audience. She waved.

"Still draw ladies like bees to a flower, huh?" AJ commented.

Danny didn't answer and didn't wave back to Clover. While he was confident he had his timing back, he wanted to work on his form. He had at least two, probably three more rides on the bull before they needed to call it quits.

Danny blanked out the fact that Clover was there and focused on the bull's tuft of hair again. He mentally went over the last ride and the animal's quirks. He'd go for the tip of the hat, one of his signature moves that audiences loved and expected from him.

He nodded his head to AJ to let the animal out and Black Fury tore out of the chute, racing forward before going into a series of hard bucks and sharp turns. Danny found his rhythm, and as he counted to the six-second mark, he reached for his hat. But Black Fury went into a fast spin—the move he never did. Danny tried to tighten his grip as well as find his center. His hand was numb. He couldn't move his fingers. He let the hat fly as he reached down to loosen the rope so he could get off the bull fast. The animal reversed his spin and Danny went soaring off the animal, landing hard, his deadened right hand and rapidly numbing arm crumpling under him.

CLOVER'S HEART STUTTERED as Danny flew through the air then stopped when his arm collapsed under him and his head smacked onto the dirt. He didn't pop up immediately. She ran from the stands, ignoring the ankle-breaking unevenness of the dirt to reach him. Two other men were already there. "Danny," she yelled. "Danny."

He didn't answer and the men didn't even turn to look at her. This was bad. She searched for her phone in her purse as she ran forward. The men moved and she saw that Danny was sitting up. Thank God. His arm looked odd. Had he broken it?

"I want to go again," Danny said. "Just caught me off guard with that spin."

"His spin is more like a slow turn in a cul-de-sac," AJ said. She remembered him from her days on the junior bull-riding circuit.

"Is your arm broken? How many fingers do you see?" she asked, elbowing past the men.

"What the hell are you doing here?" Danny asked, the new knot on his forehead looking worse with his frown.

"Was looking at some land out this way and wondered what the commotion was," she lied. Danny's frown deepened. "Let me call 911. You probably have a concussion."

"I don't have a damned concussion and my arm is fine."

She could see the arm wasn't fine. It hung at the wrong angle with his fingers clawed inward. She reached out to touch it and he didn't move away. "What's wrong?" She was worried. Had he broken his arm? Put it out of joint?

"Damn it, woman. I'm fine." He pushed himself up with his good hand and stood. Neither of the other men said anything as he rubbed at his dangling arm. It didn't move or jerk. That had to mean it wasn't broken. He couldn't do that with a broken bone, could he?

The older man said, "That's enough for today."

"That bull's got at least two more rides in him."

AJ put his hand on Danny's shoulder. "If Dave says we're done, then we're done."

Danny stiffened except for that dangling right arm.

Had he injured his back? Was he paralyzed? "Danny, I'm taking you to the hospital right now if you won't let me call 911. Or what about Pepper? I'll call her."

He knocked the phone from her hand. "I said no," he shouted. Everyone froze, including the bull.

"What the hell, man?" AJ said. "You need to apologize."

Danny kept his back to her. "Sorry."

"Lame," AJ muttered.

Danny whipped around, his arm swinging and his face dark with anger and fear. "I'm sorry, m'lady. I shouldn't have hit your phone. I shouldn't have yelled." He stomped off.

"Aren't you going after him? He hurt himself," Clover pointed out to the men.

AJ answered, "Bull riders hurt themselves all the time."

She snorted and hurried after Danny. She knew riders hurt themselves, but this was bad. Between his head and arm, he shouldn't be driving. She caught up with him just feet from his pickup.

"Danny." He stopped but didn't turn to her. "At least go see Pepper. Your arm looks bad."

"Enough," he whispered hoarsely. "I don't need you acting like you care."

That hurt. "I care about you, Danny." She tentatively touched his shoulder, approaching him like she would a hurting horse.

"Ha. You're trying to destroy me and my town."

She'd chalk that up to his pain. "Regardless, you're a human being, and it's obvious that something happened to you in that fall."

"Nothing more than usual."

"Turn around and talk to me. I know you're stubborn, but I never knew you to be stupid."

His shoulders dropped a fraction of an inch and he turned. His face was anguished.

"Danny," she whispered, "what's wrong? Let me—"

"It's numb. It may never get better."

"Your arm?"

He nodded. "The doctors said that it's probably a nerve that's inflamed. Probably. When it…well, when it acts up, my arm goes numb. My fingers are numb a lot but that's not so bad. Have to be careful with the saw, though." He laughed hollowly.

Words fled from her and she just wanted to enfold him in her arms. She was woman enough to know he wouldn't allow that. "I hadn't heard. How do you expect to ride?"

"I've ridden with worse. I can do this."

She wouldn't point out that had been stupid. "I know doctors in New York and San Antonio. I could talk to them."

"I've seen enough doctors. I'll do this show because that's what I said I'd do. It's going to raise tens of thousands of dollars for the garden. I can't let Angel Crossing down."

"But you could—"

"I'll be fine. Plus, you and your daddy will be gone by then. Destroyed our town and moved on."

"I never took you for a drama king," Clover said, not sure exactly how much of that was teasing.

"I don't need this crap."

She touched his good arm. "It's my turn to apologize. At least let me drive you home."

"I told you I'm fine."

"Yeah, right. I can see the knot on your forehead. I'll follow you, then."

He didn't say anything but got in his truck. She hurried to her rental to follow him. She wasn't done with convincing him to go see Pepper or head to the emergency room. She knew how bull riders were—as stubborn as the animals they rode.

THEY HAD TAKEN the puppies and Maggie May out and rounded them back up and into the apartment without a word between them.

"I've got people adopting all but Hulk and Maggie May," he said when they got back to the apartment.

"You're keeping them? What about your landlord?"

He shook his head and stopped abruptly.

"That's it. Sit and let me look at your head and arm. I see your hair has grown in over the stitches just fine." Thinking of Danny hurt made her stomach clench with fear.

"I'm not a little boy," he said, plopping down in a chair.

She pushed back the blond hair with streaks of near white from being hatless in the sun. The lump had a small bruise in the center. That needed ice. Even she knew that. She reached down for his right arm and he moved his shoulder to keep her from touching him. "I need to make sure you didn't hurt it. You wouldn't know since you can't feel it."

He turned his head away from her but she could see his jaw moving with anger and frustration.

She carefully and slowly took his arm, treating him like a skittish stallion who needed his hooves cleaned. She smiled at that. Danny would like being compared to a stallion over a bull. She worked the plaid sleeve of his shirt up his forearm. The skin looked fine. She ran her hands along it and couldn't feel any lumps or bumps. His hand looked fine, too. Could the odd angle she'd noticed been all because of the numbness? She couldn't push the sleeve beyond the elbow, so she'd have to take off his shirt. His face was still turned away. *Pretend you're Pepper examining a patient.* She started at the button at his neck. Now he turned his head.

"What the hell are you doing?"

"I need to look at your whole arm." She kept her voice steady and unemotional.

"I'll do it." He stood and yanked off the shirt clumsily.

Clover focused on his right arm. She reached deep to touch him without emotion. Her hand started at his shoulder, well muscled and strong. Everything good there. Her hand inched down onto his bicep, which jerked. She glanced up at him, but his face hadn't changed from its stoic cowboy lines. She massaged down the muscle, feeling for anything that shouldn't be there. The skin was warm and taut with a spring that reminded her of their nights together, her fingers digging into those same arms and holding on.

"I've never had an exam like that," Danny said as he looked at where her hands stroked his bicep. His smile was cocky.

She stilled her fingers, even as they ached to sink into his flesh to feel the heated strength of him. "You seem okay, but you should still see Pepper."

"I don't think her exam will be the same."

"Stop being such a jerk." She stepped away from

him. The warm bubble that had surrounded them as she'd checked his arm had burst with his stupid comments. Time for her to go.

"I'm sorry," he said suddenly. "My mama taught me better. I appreciate your checking on me."

She nodded, not able to speak because she was so off balance. She was getting whiplash from his shifting mood. "I'm glad you really are fine, except for the numbness." Now they were back to stoic cowboy.

"There is that. I'll be practicing more with my left."

She'd been dismissed again. She'd take the hint this time. "I'm glad to hear that the puppies have homes."

"All but Hulk."

"He's a cutie, though. I can't imagine it will take long."

"Maybe. Except he may be deaf. That's sometimes the case with white dogs. It's hard to say."

"Poor little guy," she said as she looked over at the puppy pen, where everyone was sleeping peacefully.

"Yeah." Danny's shoulders slumped with…weariness, fear, sadness? She couldn't be sure. She was a glutton for punishment because she stepped to him and picked up his bad right hand, giving it a squeeze even if he couldn't feel it. He stiffened for a moment, and then she was in his arms, his lips on hers devouring her and heating her.

Chapter Eleven

Danny wasn't sure if he'd slept. The evening and night were a haze of loving Clover. Now it was morning and only one beam of the rising sun crept through the crack in the curtain. He couldn't deny that a new day had dawned. Maggie May had yipped twice to be let out. He slid from the bed so he wouldn't wake Clover. Her mass of auburn hair sparked red in the light. He wanted to bury his face again in its softly fragrant length.

He had responsibilities. She would wake soon enough and realize that they had made another mistake, except it didn't feel like a mistake. That aching emptiness he'd been trying to fill with Angel Crossing and its problems had been gone in her arms. Even now that space had a fullness he hadn't felt since…he'd been a teen and trembling with his love and need for her. Dangerous thoughts and imaginings. She was going to destroy what he'd built for himself here.

He kept moving. He'd learned that was the best way to deal with pain, just keep moving and don't think. He got Maggie May and the puppies outside with no accidents. He allowed them to romp longer than usual, telling himself they needed the extra exercise, not that he was hoping Clover would sneak away and he wouldn't have to face her. Now the canine family stood at the bottom of the stairs waiting for him. No more stalling. When he got them all adopted, he'd miss this in the mornings. But it was best for them. They couldn't live in an apartment, especially with his busy schedule. He didn't have the time for training a puppy or a new dog.

He herded them up the stairs. The door opened and Clover appeared in yesterday's clothes, her hair shining in the sun and her expression in shadow. His face felt numb today. He couldn't make it move in any way that made sense. He looked down at the boards of the landing. Better than trying to control his stiff features or seeing the regret in her eyes.

"I wanted to make sure your arm's okay," she said as he brushed by her and inside.

The reason she'd stayed. Pity. "Good enough to take care of myself."

"Don't be so sensitive," she said. "I didn't mean anything."

"Thanks for letting me know what last night was about. Helping the cripple feel better about himself."

He went to the dog food bowls. Why didn't she leave?

"The puppies and Maggie May will be leaving soon?"

"Yes." The dogs crowded him as he put down their food. Time to refill the water.

"You'll miss them?"

That didn't deserve an answer. He didn't have a choice, like he hadn't about his career or about being mayor.

She went on when he didn't answer. "Do you need help paying the vet bills?"

"Just because I'm not riding anymore doesn't mean—"

"Jeez. You're as prickly as a cactus in May."

"What?"

"You used to say that."

He may have. It was one of the many sayings from his mother that made as much sense as a cowboy in heels. "My mama said that. She says a lot of things that don't really make sense."

"I did wonder. But it sounds good, doesn't it? Should I make us coffee?"

Why did the thought of sitting down and having coffee with Clover seem like the absolute best way to start the morning? Because this woman had always made him feel that way. He had never been sure around her, like he was with other women or even around ornery bulls. "Sure," he said. "I don't think I have much for breakfast. I can run down to the diner." How would he explain an order that would probably include yogurt or fruit or something like that? Everyone in the diner would know what he'd been up to.

"Coffee will do for now." She turned from him and went into the kitchen. He stood for a moment, watching her, and the unsteady feeling was gone. This felt right, a morning routine and a little conversation. He'd had a girlfriend or three over the years and this time of day had never felt like this. What was it about Clover?

"Black with sugar, right?" she asked over her shoulder.

He went to her and wrapped his arms around her, burying his face in the crook of her neck because he wanted her right now. He couldn't wait and he didn't want to think about why.

"Oh, my," she said. "Someone doesn't need a cup of coffee to wake up."

HE AND CLOVER had spent the past two weeks looking for homes for Maggie May and Hulk. So, of course, that meant spending a lot of time together, both in and out of bed. She'd gone to the arena with him as he continued to work on his riding, not saying anything when he ate dirt regularly. She'd even helped him with his strength training and cardio with jogs through the streets. He knew the town had taken note. He'd gotten looks from Irvin and Loretta that said, *What are you doing, boy?* Bobby Ames had straight-out asked if he believed fraternizing with a VCW representative would get him a better price for his properties. Danny had barely stopped himself from punching the man.

He and Clover stood in the parking lot behind Angel Crossing's main street, which also served as the town's outdoor farmers' market. They'd just sent off another puppy to one of the homes he'd found. The family had two kids and everyone looked so excited. Maggie May and Hulk were still with him. He knew Maggie May would be tough to place and had hoped that AJ would take her as a friend for Butch. Danny knew most people wanted puppies, not full-grown mutts. He'd been working with her, though. Teaching her commands to make her more attractive to a family or even an older person looking for a companion. As smart as she was, he'd bet he could teach her to get the remote and turn on the lights. Hulk, the little runt, was deaf in one ear with only a little bit of hearing in the other. Danny was teaching him hand signals, and like Maggie May, he picked them up quickly.

"I know that she'll be happy, but I'm still—"

Danny pulled Clover into an embrace. She'd cried each time they'd placed one of the pups in a new home. "You can't have a dog and neither can I. The kids looked so excited. She'll do well. I gave them my number in case there's any problems. I told them they could call me and I'd come get her, no questions asked."

She hugged him harder and whispered her thanks. Nearly as good as winning a buckle and the money. Damn. He was getting in deep with Clover. Two more weeks until the big meeting, the final decision on Rico Pueblo having been postponed at the last council meeting. The one he should be preparing for, instead of worrying about puppies and Clover's feelings.

"I knew there was something special about you when we first met."

"It was my butt in my jeans. That's what you told me."

"That was good, too. But I saw the way you treated that ragged dog you had. You never yelled at him, even when he chewed up your new belt."

"Jack was a piece of work. I had that belt specially made and had only worn it once."

She looked up at him, her blue eyes shining with more than tears, and he couldn't imagine how he'd live up to what she thought he was. "You even told your sister Jessie to stop teasing me."

"I knew what it was like to be in her crosshairs," he said lightly.

"Now look at you, trying to save a town and a bunch of puppies." She pulled his head down and kissed him hard. "Why do you have to be so sweet? Why did I think you weren't worth my time back then?"

"I wasn't and I'm not," he said, trying to put a little distance between them. "I was young, innocent when we met. A lot has happened since then."

"To both of us, but you haven't changed that much. You still have a great butt," she said with a laugh. "Even better," she whispered softly into his ear, "you've learned how to… You're a good lover, generous, kind, caring."

"It's you. You make me that way. No one else… Let me just say that it's special." Crap. Why had he confessed that?

She kissed him again, her lips softly nibbling at his as she held him to her. Her curves so familiar that his hand settled into her waist like a chicken coming home to roost. He laughed against her lips. Happy.

"What?" she asked, her blue eyes unfocused.

"Nothing. Let's go home." He didn't think what he meant by that.

"Yes. Maggie May and Hulk are waiting for us."

Their hips bumped companionably against each other as they strolled to his apartment, his arm thrown over her shoulder. No point in thinking too hard about why he could imagine doing the same thing every day for the rest of his life.

CLOVER STIRRED AS the puppy's whine went from pathetic to a baying howl.

"Shh." She heard Danny and his "stealthy" footsteps. "Don't wake your mama."

Her heart stopped then cracked open. Danny had loved her last night well and truly but that wasn't what made her want him. This early-morning stealth and his comments were what had wormed themselves into her heart. She feared this would make her want to stay in Angel Crossing and give up on her dream. Just like when she'd met him the first time. She'd fallen hard for him and wanted to give up on college to be with him while he competed. He'd been on his way even then. She would have given it all up and gladly. But going back to her "real" life and eventually seeing pictures of Danny with another girl had convinced her that her future lay elsewhere. She had to remember that again. She'd nearly gained the position she'd fought for. The one that she'd gone to Wharton for, the one that her ability with numbers should have gotten her over her brother years ago.

But when she started thinking about the future, she had doubts, worries and fears. That was normal. Then Danny would kiss the nape of her neck, making her shudder all over. Her dreams would shift. She'd see herself with him and with their babies. She'd never imagined herself with children. Her life was going to be all about her work.

A puppy growl reached her as did Danny's attempt to quiet Hulk. She could put off for another day making decisions about the rest of her life. She didn't need to understand statistics to know the likelihood of her and Danny staying together made for a bad bet.

Two HOURS LATER, she'd done a week's worth of deep breathing after finding the hole the puppy had chewed in her new Coach bag. Despite her early-morning dreams of a life with Danny, she was on her way to meet with

Melvin about a tract of property he owned just outside of town. VCW wanted it as part of Rico Pueblo.

Her father had decided to stay until the next council meeting two weeks from now. He'd set up a satellite office in one of the properties they owned along Miner's Gulch. Danny had even helped fit it out to make it usable.

The different parts of her life were beginning to blur. She hadn't figured out if that was a good or a bad thing…yet. She had two more weeks to make that decision. Well, hell, there was Danny's pickup. What was he doing out here? He'd better be bidding on a rehab job and not talking to the man about his property.

The long, low ranch house had a history to it and amazing views of the surrounding mountains. Well, history for Arizona. In New York, it would be just a pup of a house. A back part of it was old-time adobe. Too bad the house and the barns would be flattened for VCW's plans. Sometimes you had to break a few eggs. Or something like that. Clover knocked on the door as she rubbed each boot against the back of her jeans. Not something her mother or father would approve of, but in dusty Arizona, it was a must to keep her pink cowgirl boots looking decent. Today she'd dressed not to impress or intimidate, but to prove that she wasn't so different from the residents of Angel Crossing—jeans, plaid shirt (one of her mother's designs in pink and purple, highlighted with silver lamé), white hat with a dyed pink snake band and her pink boots. Feminine and Western. She looked good.

"Hello, Melvin, good to see you again," she said to the balding man with the thick waist and short legs. "I hope I'm not disturbing your talk with the mayor." No use pretending she didn't know who was here.

"Seems everyone wants to visit today. Even your daddy is here."

She smiled because otherwise her mouth would have dropped open. What was her father doing here? Had he hidden his car on purpose? She'd told him she'd take care of this. She'd spoken to Melvin at least four times about the property, the price, the contingencies. Today she was going to close the deal and get his name on the sale papers, which would give her plenty of time to finish the transfer before the meeting. She wanted this property to be the cornerstone of the portion of the Rico Peublo single-family home development that mixed history and nature, in the form of world-class views.

"We're out back. Come along. I never would have guessed this dry old ranch would be worth so much."

Crap. The man saw dollar signs, always bad for making the budget work. Clover smiled again. That was what a lady did when she didn't agree and needed to keep her mouth shut. She wanted to figure out exactly what was going on before she said anything more.

They walked around the outside of the house, entering a garden and patio protected by a wooden gate that looked even older than the house and included a crude carving of something that might be an angel.

"Daddy," Clover said.

Her father nodded at her and Danny gave her a blank-eyed stare. What the heck was going on?

"Take a seat," Melvin said as he sat down in a large wooden chair with more angels carved on the arms and back, similar to that on the gate. "Growing up here, I never could have imagined anyone would be so interested in my ranch, and now I have three buyers."

"Two," Clover corrected, settling herself. She would

speak calmly with this man who held a lot of the cards right now. "I also work for VCW."

"Yep, but there must be some kind of insider trading or something since there are two of you here." The man was absolutely gleeful.

"I assure you that VCW has a very clear plan for this and the additional properties that we have acquired."

Danny said, "Melvin, you've lived here your entire life, and it was your great-grandfather who built the ranch and founded the town. Do you think a company from New York City will treat you and Angel Crossing right?"

"If they give me the money I want, I'll be treated right."

Clover knew it. This was all about money. She'd found that a lot of life came down to money. At least for her parents it had. They'd never officially divorced because it would cost too much. Each continued to grow their business and ignore that they were still hitched to another human.

"I believe," her father said smoothly, "that we had a very advantageous agreement."

"Probably." Melvin stalled. "But I want to hear what the mayor and your daughter have to offer."

"I'm not bidding against my own company," she said, dismayed that her father had stepped into the fray.

"I'm only out here to make the offer you should have and clean up your mess," her father said to her in a low tone that she hoped Melvin couldn't hear.

She was more than annoyed. She'd been near to completing a deal with Melvin. She'd even been toying with the idea of keeping elements from the old ranch as part of an entrance to the development, hoping it would bring down his price.

"What about you, Mayor? Going to up your price?" Melvin asked.

Danny's expression froze and his fingers drummed against his leg. "You know I don't have anything more to offer and this property is worth less than we offered. At this rate, I'm going to end up back at the rodeo to make money."

"Don't care about you and the bull riding. This property is worth whatever anyone is willing to pay, not what the county has on that piece of paper. Your sister and her archaeologist have said that there could be 'significant historical meaning to the property as well as evidence of presettlement materials.' That should be worth some coin."

Danny stood, his blue eyes cool as his gaze landed on Clover before he spoke to Melvin. "I gave you the offer and explained why your property is important to Angel Crossing. I can't do more than that."

She hesitated for a moment and followed Danny out. "This is just business."

"Dirty business," he countered. He took in a deep breath and blew it out. "Like I said, it might be that I'm not meant to be a developer or a mayor, that my place is on the back of a bull."

"Danny, I—" What could she say? That she didn't want him to ride bulls again because it was too dangerous? She didn't have any right to say that. "Sorry about the property." She turned and walked back into the house.

"We have an agreement, then?" her father asked Melvin.

"Maybe. I'll need to think on it now that I've got so many people interested and know that there might be some ancient artifacts underground."

"The only ancient artifact that you should be looking for is your integrity," Clover said, glaring at her father as she walked out again. She wouldn't think about why she'd been more upset about Danny's crazy idea about bull riding than her father stepping in to take over her project.

Chapter Twelve

After the meeting with Melvin, Danny couldn't speak with Clover. He couldn't ignore she was in competition with him for his town—even though that sounded pompous and asinine. He didn't have a problem with the company presenting its vision to the council. That was fair. But now her father was using cash to get his way. Danny had seen how much Melvin had been offered—twice the value of the property with extra for resettlement. Losing the ranch, though, would be losing a part of Angel Crossing's heritage. Lavonda's husband would prove that. He'd already poked around and found archaeological evidence of pre-Spanish settlement.

Today he and Clover were supposed to have met potential adopters for Hulk. Clover had texted him twenty minutes before the meeting that she couldn't come. She hadn't even given him an excuse. Even if he didn't want to see her or speak with her, he'd thought she'd cared about the little puppy. Apparently, she'd just been passing the time until she and her father threw around their millions. They'd even been after Pepper to sell them the old theater so it could be torn down and replaced with a state-of-the-art IMAX theater that would take people on virtual tours of the Grand Canyon. They were in Arizona. Just go to the blasted Grand Canyon, if you wanted to see it.

What a day. Hulk's adopters hadn't worked out, he had a lull in his business and his plan was ready to go belly-up. He went to the diner, hoping for a little food but, more important, hoping that he'd see people who had some influence over other Angelites and even the council. It was a long shot that he'd see anyone like that or that they'd want to talk with him. Everyone was getting a little tired of the discussion.

"You just missed your girlfriend," Marlena, the waitress, said as he walked in. Others nodded hello to him.

"She's not my girlfriend."

"Could have fooled me, considering I saw her coming out of your apartment in the morning."

No use denying it. Plus, he had a greater purpose, as they say. "Just here for coffee and pie."

"No pie. Got some of those doughnuts that get delivered."

The doughnuts were awful. "Just coffee." He looked around for someone he could persuade to join his cause.

"Why aren't you at the Hendersons'?" his sister Lavonda asked from behind him, giving him a start.

"Waiting for a tile shipment. Where did you come from?"

Lavonda opened, then closed her mouth, then opened it again. "We're in the back room."

He'd heard about the room and the women, aka the Devil's Food Diner Back Room Mafia. A group of ladies who spun yarn, knit and ran the town (according to them). "Who are you trying to match up now?"

The group had convinced Pepper that she should take on AJ and his daughter months ago.

"We're not a matchmaker club. We're working on a business plan for Sylvia. She's looking at starting an apiary in the community garden. Honey and beeswax are hot items right now."

"Won't have that if Clover and her daddy get their way." They wanted Wild West modern, which Danny imagined was like plopping Phoenix down into Angel Crossing.

"Is Clover there with you now?" he asked.

"Don't act like lions and puppies are lying down together. She's got ideas for the town. We wanted to hear them firsthand before the meeting. Plus, we heard about Melvin and his place. We wanted to ask her about that, too. You know Jones has explored there for his... Let's just say the place might be related to his research."

Danny couldn't puzzle out what his sister was not saying because of the angry roaring in his ears. How dare Clover come in here and act like she was the savior? He would go in there and set her and the Back Room Mafia straight.

"She's going to destroy the town," he said as he wrenched open a door. It would have made more of an impression if it hadn't led to the storage closet. "Damn it."

Lavonda said, "The next door on the right." He didn't turn. He didn't need to to know she was laughing at him. His neck burned with embarrassment. He yanked open the next door over and said, "Clover Van Camp is here to destroy Angel Crossing."

"Wow," said Marie, her round, wrinkled face grinning. "I didn't know she had so much power. We'll start calling her Clover-zilla. Wait. Wasn't there a monster movie called *Cloverfield*?"

"Not much of a movie," another woman said as she clacked away with two needles. "I like Clover-zilla. Now, that would be a movie. What do you think, Doris?"

Another woman with one flashing hooked needle nodded. "There are a couple of places I'd like to see blown up. Wait. Is that her superpower?"

"They'll get rid of the diner and charge you to have your meetings," he said, guessing that would be true under VCW. The plan was about making money, not a community. He looked around the table, making sure his gaze didn't land on Clover.

"The diner's nearly killed half the town at one time or another. Now they don't even have pie," Marie said. "The man making the desserts quit, or Chief Rudy suggested he move on. Something about counterfeit something or other."

"Danny," Clover said loudly enough that it cut through the "remember who used to live where" conversation around the table. "I'm just here to visit and answer questions."

"Do they know that your company plans to tear down most of the town, including Melvin's place, and put up condos?"

"We've talked about the housing. Not having to care for a yard sounds good to some residents," she said.

She just didn't get it. He knew what she and her father were planning. No matter what kind of lipstick you put on that porcupine, it would still stick it to you. "What about the cost? Did you tell them about that?"

"I'm answering questions. Not making a presentation. We'll do that at the meeting."

"Will it be everything you have mapped out? That you're going to make this an exclusive community, put a gate up?"

"It's going to be just what I talked about. If you think that's exclusive, then okay."

"That's enough, Danny," his sister said. "We all know you're mayor and you have your own plan. We've heard about it from you often enough."

"She's lying to you," he said, not willing to let this go. "She and her father are selling everyone a bill of goods."

"I am not lying," Clover said, standing. "I don't lie. Unlike you."

"Me?"

"Yes, you. You act like a stand-up cowboy. You act like what you're doing is best for Angel Crossing. It's not. It'll put money in your pocket so you can leave. Isn't that what you really want to do? Leave here and go back on the road. Isn't that what SAC is all about? Aren't you going to invite everyone to see you ride again so you can get sponsors?"

As he'd been working the bulls and training, he realized that having one gimpy arm wasn't as much of a handicap as he'd imagined. Recently, with VCW putting a wrench in his future, he figured he could still have a rehab business in Angel Crossing or Tucson, while he went back on the riding circuit. He'd hire a crew to do the work, checking on them between shows.

"Have you told Mama you want to ride again?" Lavonda asked, treating him like he was twelve.

"I don't need her permission or yours. In fact, I don't need anyone's permission to make decisions about my life."

"Right. Just walk away," Clover said, leaning forward. "What do you care? You'll get what you want. You'll smile and shake hands and walk away. You never cared anyway. This was all for fun. Or wait. Not for fun—it stroked your ego, and God knows you've got a big one of those."

"You didn't seem to mind 'stroking my ego.'"

A gasp went through the room and Clover stepped back like she'd been slapped.

"Danforth Clayton Leigh—" Lavonda said.

Before she could say she was disappointed in him, he went on. "I want to tell the truth. Isn't that what we're doing here? We had a good time but it's over. Just like that summer. I was some dumb cowboy that was available. I'm not so dumb anymore. I've learned a lot, including when to walk away."

CLOVER CHECKED HER suit one last time in the mirror over the bathroom sink in Dead Man's Cottage. She'd be out of here soon and back to New York with CFO as her title. If she said it often enough, it would be true. There wasn't an iota of the Texas beauty queen or the cowgirl who'd fallen for a bull rider with a bad arm. In the mirror was Clover Van Camp, an executive ready to break balls and build empires. Tonight at the town-council meeting of Angel Crossing, Arizona, her real career would begin. Her mother had called today, the first she'd heard from her since Clover had walked away from fashion and from the life her mother had dreamed would make Clover happy. She'd been so wrong.

Apparently, her mother had heard about the meeting. She'd also known about Rico Pueblo. She couldn't imagine her parents speaking about anything other than how horrible the other was. In any case, she'd told her mother she'd found her true calling, making the numbers and projects work for VCW.

"Cowgirls Don't Cry" rang out from her phone. Lavonda was calling. Clover hesitated, then picked up. The other woman had been friendly and sympathetic enough earlier.

"Are you ready?" she asked. "Jones is going to wear a kilt."

The non sequitur threw Clover for a moment. "Thanks for the heads-up. I've got my presentation memorized and I'm out the door right now."

"Pepper's mother is coming, too. Have you met Faye? She's a hoot and a half. She says Danny is a Taurus just like AJ. I'm not sure what that has to do with his plans, but that's Faye."

"Is the whole town coming out?"

"Nearly. Anita and Rita are even closing Jim's. Everyone, me included, wants to hear the whole plan again and see how council votes."

Clover got in the car, reminding herself that presenting to the council was no more intimidating than walking across a stage in a bathing suit. "I've got to go. I don't want to get pulled over for driving and talking."

CLOVER SAW HER father outside the town hall. He was on his phone and waved her away. She'd meet him inside. She knew what she had to do. He was here just to observe, despite what had happened at Melvin's. She went over the numbers in her head and quickly reviewed the bullet points. She'd blow the council and Danny out of the water with her grasp of the numbers. There would be no way for them to say no. She'd counter every possible argument. Having the time to stay in Angel Crossing had been a big help. She'd begun to understand the town and that had made the tweaks to her presentation even more compelling.

She was sorry that her success meant Danny would lose out, but that was the way of life. There were always winners and losers. She was going to be on the winning side this time. Plus, he was going back to the rodeo—that had become obvious. She didn't care what he did. He'd been a blip in her life, like he'd been that summer. Good to look back on as a fond memory and nothing more.

She walked into the packed room and saw two empty seats at the front. Those were for her and her father, she guessed. She kept her head up to match her confident strides. Tonight she'd be a winner in more ways than one. She'd finally get the job she should have had and she'd be moving on from Angel Crossing. After tonight, her life would really start. Everything that she'd been doing up until now had just been a prelude to her real work and life.

She pulled out the newly printed materials for the council and put one package at each of the places, including the mayor's. None of the members had been seated. That was unusual. And where was her father? They had exactly seven minutes until the start of the meeting.

"Oh, my," she heard a woman whisper, and she turned to look for Danny arriving. Instead, it was a tall man with auburn hair, wearing a kilt. On his right was Lavonda, looking tiny and happy. She waved at Clover as they took two of the few remaining seats. Pepper was there along with AJ and a woman who must be Pepper's mother.

Clover refused to check her watch again. She sat quietly, waiting. Waiting for the rest of her life to start.

Where was everyone?

As soon as she landed in New York, she'd look for a bigger apartment. With her salary as CFO, she could find a nice place, one that took dogs—which her current place didn't—because she thought she'd need a canine. It would be good for her health. There'd been studies—

Crack. "I call the meeting to order," Bobby Ames said, slamming down his gavel a second time.

When and how had the entire council, including Danny, come into the room without her noticing? Crap. She had to get her head back in the game. One more time through the bullet points as Bobby Ames explained the agenda for the meeting.

Where was her father? He should be here to see this. It was a project that would open new opportunities for VCW, usher in a new era. That was the speech she planned for the company's board when she got back to New York.

"We're ready for the vote," Bobby Ames said.

Before Clover could protest, Danny and a quarter of the audience shouted out.

Bobby pounded his gavel until there was quiet. "We had an executive session before the meeting to review new information. It seems Van Camp has expanded the scope of its work and will be assuring the town double its current property taxes as well as a substantial donation to the library and recreation funds. There is also talk of a fund for the garden."

Clover didn't allow herself to smile in triumph. So what if her father swooped in and took over the project. It sounded like he'd gotten the council to agree to what they were proposing and better for Angel Crossing. She was a little...hurt—that was probably the best word—that he hadn't included her on the negotiations. Did it really matter if they got the go-ahead?

"We can't be bought," Danny said, and two or three people, including his sister, agreed from the audience.

"We were elected to do what was best for the town. This is the best," said Irvin Miller.

"What about maintaining our independence? You know that money's got to have strings," Danny said. "Van Camp thinks we're just a bunch of dumb hicks."

"Mayor," Bobby said, "this is a good plan and your opinion might be a bit biased considering your property will no longer be eligible for residential development."

"Sounds like hooey to me," Anita said. "What about me? I've been paying taxes for years and what am I going to get out of the deal?"

"Yeah," said Rita. "Remember the mayor got us that money for the market and to save the theater? Will they keep that and all of the farm plots in town?"

More people from the audience spoke up now about what was working with the town. Clover needed to step in. Somehow the tide was beginning to shift despite Bobby's liberal use of the gavel.

"I'd like to address your concerns, if I may, Mr. President." She smiled brightly at Bobby Ames. "I've been in Angel Crossing for a few months now, speaking with residents, business owners and anyone who will listen. What I've discovered is a town with a lot of heart and creativity. You've all worked hard to keep your town from dying. You've helped each other and lent a hand. Now it's time for you to benefit from all of that work. Van Camp Worldwide can be the partner to bring prosperity and jobs. To make sure your sons and daughters want to call Rico Pueblo home, too. I know the mayor has been one of your town's greatest advocates and his ideas had merit. But now you can see that VCW will make your town more than just a place to survive but one where you'll thrive." She saw heads nodding. She'd gotten the crowd back on her side.

"You think you know what's best for us, Clover Van Camp. You and your New York daddy? You're just a rodeo beauty queen who's lost her crown."

"Danny—" Lavonda started.

Clover didn't turn. Her gaze stayed on Danny. If he was prepared to fight dirty, so was she. "Those are big words from a bull rider who gave up because he was scared."

"I gave up bull riding because I became mayor."

"No, you didn't. You gave it up because you were afraid that a little damage to your arm was the end of your glory days and that you might actually have to work at winning those purses." The air was sucked out of the room and Danny's gaze went dark with an emotion she couldn't name. "I may not be a beauty queen anymore but I don't rely on people remembering that I once had a crown to make myself feel good.

I don't come up with a plan to make a town feel grateful to me for just being there. And I certainly don't make anyone feel guilty for having a dream beyond the dust and dirt of a bull-riding arena. Angel Crossing doesn't need you as much as you need it, Danny. They'll be proving it by accepting VCW's offer."

Clover didn't move her gaze from Danny's and didn't acknowledge the glare she could feel from his sister. In the end, VCW's request was accepted and her father showed up just as she was having her picture taken for a business blog.

"Good job," he said. "I've got the demolition crews set up for next week, and the lawyers have the eviction notices all drawn up."

Chapter Thirteen

Danny watched everyone file out of the meeting and saw that his sister and brother-in-law hadn't left. He wanted them to leave. He didn't want to speak with anyone. He didn't want to be a pathetic mess, punching a wall or wailing like a baby. Between losing his chance at changing Angel Crossing for the better and Clover's revealing his secret to the town and his family—the same thing, really—he wanted to crawl under a rock. He wished he was a hard-drinking, drown-his-sorrows-in-a-beer cowboy. He'd just never had many sorrows. He was making up for that now. He glared at Lavonda, telling her telepathically to get the hell out. She just gave him an indulgent smile—that was the trouble with being the youngest.

"Clover's plan will be good for *your* business," Danny said to his sister after strolling nonchalantly through the empty chamber.

"Possibly, although Jones isn't happy about what Melvin's doing." Lavonda's gaze didn't stray from Danny's face. "We'll talk about your bull riding later, with Mama and Jessie."

"There are artifacts on that property," Jones said, his Scottish accent not out of place with the kilt. "I told him that we could add his ranch to our tour and give him a percentage of our revenue."

"Can't you still do that?" Danny asked.

"Not once Van Camp starts its work. They have plans for that property to be a huge gated community. You know Melvin's property has some of the best views," Lavonda said.

"I was at Melvin's when Clover and Heyer, Clover's father, were there. I didn't know they wanted to put up gates, though." Danny was proud he hadn't stumbled over *her* name.

"We should talk with the state's historic commission about Melvin's. We should be able to get a stay on the sale," Jones said, his Scottish burr more obvious.

Danny had stopped listening because what had happened hit him in the face. He'd lost. His plan was done. He owned property that had worth only to VCW and all of his savings were tied up in it. He needed to move on. Angel Crossing had decided what they wanted and it wasn't him.

"Finally sunk in, huh?" Lavonda said, reaching out slowly to touch his arm. He jerked away.

"I've got a lot to do. I'll have to see what Van Camp will give me for my properties. If they don't pay well, I'll be stuck. It's time for me to come out of retirement anyway."

"What? Wait. You're really going to ride again?" Lavonda asked, her voice rising. Jones put a large hand on her shoulder. Danny's gut fell. That was the kind of gesture a couple made for each other without thinking. The kind of gesture that could turn a bad situation into something tolerable.

"There's not enough work here for me. I don't think

Rico Pueblo will want me for mayor. Anyway, I'm a cowboy…a bull rider." Saying the words didn't feel as right as he'd hoped. "Gotta get home and let the dogs out." Danny made sure he sauntered from the building and strolled down the street. He was cool with what had happened. Sure. Initially it had been a slap in the face. Now that he thought on it, the whole situation was good. He'd never planned to settle in Angel Crossing. When he'd landed in the town, he was just waiting until his arm healed. So maybe it'd never heal entirely—that didn't mean he needed to stop riding. Like Pepper's mother, Faye, would say, this was the universe's way of telling him that he needed to change his path. He just wished the universe hadn't had to do its talking in front of the whole town.

THE FAMILY WHO said they'd take on Hulk met him in the Angel Crossing all-purpose lot. They had two children, one of whom had a cochlear implant to help him hear, so they thought a dog with a similar challenge would be a good choice. His sister Jessie had recommended them. The son had been in one of her therapeutic riding camps at Hope's Ride. She'd vouched for him and his family. They'd met on a Friday afternoon as the vendors for Saturday's farmers' market started to mark out their stalls in the lot. Some would come in early tomorrow but many started their setup on Fridays. Not everyone was an early riser like Pepper, who helped organize the market.

The family got back in their dusty SUV, just as Pepper pulled up to supervise the vendors and, of course, Clover came racing toward him.

"Is he gone?" she asked.

He hadn't seen her in the week since the council meeting. He'd been busy ramping up his training regime and discussing how to get back in the bull-riding game with AJ. He hadn't talked about Clover, even when AJ had asked him about her. He'd only just prevented himself from decking the man when he'd suggested that Danny should apologize to Clover (even if Danny hadn't done anything wrong), then beg her to take him back.

Clover stood with hands on hips in front of him, her soft mouth a hard line and her blue eyes flinty. "I asked you to let me know when you found a family for Hulk."

"You told me that VCW only wanted to help Angel Crossing."

"I know...in the long run...there's always pain with change, but it will be worth it."

"Worth it. Tearing down the town, destroying what everyone has been trying to save, chasing out all of the residents will be better?" Danny wasn't worried that his voice was carrying to the vendors or to Pepper. It was all true and they should know that Clover and her company were not their savior.

"We're making things better. There will be jobs."

"What kind of jobs? And where will people live?"

"Danny," Clover said in a reasonable tone that made his head explode.

"You think you know what's best for us? You think because we live in a little town that's struggling, we should be happy for anything you're willing to offer us? We're not. We have a great town, an amazing community. That counts for a hell of a lot more than money."

"You talk a good game, but you're not staying and you didn't win the vote."

"I may not be staying, but I'm not leaving the town worse off than when I came. You and your father can't say the same thing."

"I'm not going to argue with you about this. We already did that at the meeting."

"Let's talk about the meeting." He stomped closer to her. He wanted to look her in the eye. "My hand and my arm were my business. Using them to win your case was low, even for a New York City diva. How would you like it if I aired the fact that your father has never thought you were competent enough to run any part of his business and that he came to Angel Crossing to clean up your 'mess.'" He made sure everyone heard the last sentence.

"Danny, I know you're upset but that gives you no right to treat me badly."

"You mean the way you let your daddy treat you. Please. You must like it or you would do something about it."

"I am doing something about it. I'm walking away."

"That's right," he yelled. "Run away. That's what you do best. When the going gets tough, then Clover gets going."

She turned and gave him a pitying look. What was that for? His phone pinged and he pulled it out. Hulk's new family had sent a picture of the puppy kissing the little boy. "Hell and damnation," he yelled, hurling his phone and hitting a car, dinging the door and shattering his phone.

"What bug crawled up your butt?" AJ asked as he strolled across the lot. "I see."

"What do you see?"

"An ass." AJ looked his friend up and down. "Feel better breaking your phone and putting a dent in Liddy's car? You'll owe her for that, by the way."

"I don't give a flying—"

"Don't say it, boy," Chief Rudy said. "I could hear you yelling over by Miss Faye's booth."

"Clover just left," AJ said.

"I see."

"If you *girls* think you know sh—" Danny said.

"No need for that," said the chief, who never swore. "I want you to go apologize to Liddy and promise to pay for the damage. Then you need to go speak with Miss Faye—you've upset her. Then you need to go after Clover and apologize for whatever you've done wrong."

"I have a daddy," Danny said, beyond annoyed with the two men. "I don't need you or AJ telling me what I should do. You don't see what *she's* done. *She* and Van Camp are going to ruin this town, and *she* lied about what they really have planned."

"Clover isn't the kind of woman to lie," AJ said. "She always seemed straightforward to me. I mean even back in the day. She wasn't snooty or anything. Didn't wear falsies—"

"Shut up," Danny said with a level of menace to let AJ know, friend or not, if he said another word, Danny would punch him.

"I'm not your daddy, right enough," the chief started, "but I am the law around here and there'll be no fighting, especially because you're too stubborn and bull-stupid to know you love that gal."

"Do not. It was just—" Danny stopped himself when he saw the chief's frown.

"Everyone knows it. She loves you back. And everyone knows that, too."

"Does everyone know," Danny said, "that she lied, that she's angling to be a bigwig at her daddy's business and that her idea of a perfect life is a Manhattan penthouse and a closet full of fancy purses?"

"Danny dear," Faye said, strolling up in a swirl of Stevie Nicks skirts and a cloud of patchouli. "It's always rocky when a Taurus—that's you—and a Leo get together. I told Rudy and Arthur John that before they came over. Did they explain?" she asked before going on without pause. "You need to help her with the next big decision in her life. You will be her protector by knocking all obstacles from her path and she'll calm your hot blood."

"Thank you?" Danny said, not sure what else he could answer, especially with the other two men staring at him.

"Oh, man," AJ finally said, "you are in big trouble if Faye thinks she needs to help."

"It's not me, Arthur John," she said to AJ. "It's the stars. I just interpret."

"Whatever any of you think, I am not in love with Clover."

"Yes, you are," Faye said, "and you loved Hulk. You're sad he went away today."

Danny's chest caved in with the picture in his mind of the puppy in his new home, quickly followed by the hurt on Clover's face as she left. He stared at Faye and she opened her arms. For a second, he wanted to lay his head on her shoulder and bawl like a baby. Except he was a big bad bull-riding cowboy. He didn't need to do either. "I've got work to do," he said lamely as he strode off with purpose. He certainly wasn't running. He'd made sure of that by slowing his steps to a stroll. He might not be a "drowning his sorrows in a beer" sort of cowboy, but he might change that because so far nothing else was working.

"ANOTHER BEER, ANITA," Danny said, drinking his lunch on Saturday since he wasn't hungry.

"Here you go."

He looked at the frosty mug of...root beer. "What the hell?"

"You've reached your limit, Mayor," Anita said with the sternness of a mother, one of which he already had and that was plenty.

"Two beers?"

"Yep. Heard what happened yesterday."

Great. Of course, the story had gotten around town. He never figured that the twins would turn down his business.

Anita went on. "And don't think Lem at the store will sell you liquor. I already called him."

"Tell Lavonda I don't need her to interfere."

"Didn't hear a peep from your sister."

Danny eyed Anita. Didn't look like she was lying. He put down his money and left Jim's. What was the point of being at the bar if he couldn't drink? He'd just go home and take care of his needs there. Damn.

His sisters and his baby niece stood on the sidewalk in front of him. How had they done that? Were the women in this town crazy? Something in the water? Maybe that was Clover's problem, too.

"We're taking you to lunch," Lavonda said, grabbing his arm.

"Your niece wants to have her lunch with Uncle Danny," Jessie added from his other side, her daughter settled comfortably on her hip.

He allowed them to drag him to the diner. Jessie made him sit with Gertie and help feed her.

"Here's your pie," Marlena said, setting down a slice that was covered in whipped cream, looking like a gallon had been dumped on it. "Heard about yesterday. Thought you might need extra."

"Don't get mad, Danny," Lavonda said. "Everyone feels bad about the meeting. Then you had to give up Hulk and then Clover dumped on you. I never expected that from her. She came to the Back Room."

Danny wasn't certain how being a part of the Devil's Food Diner's Back Room Mafia gave Clover Angel Crossing street cred. Was there such a thing?

"When you're done with that mountain of dessert— none of which you're going to feed to my daughter— we're going to the market," Jessie said firmly as she sipped her coffee, eyeing both him and Gertie. The little girl gave back a similarly stubborn stare.

He focused on the dessert but couldn't take a bite. He did not want to go back to the scene of the crime.

"Duncle," Gertie said. "Eat."

"I'm not hungry. Let's go play in the street."

"Danny," Jessie said. "Don't say things like that to her."

He shrugged, picked up his niece and left the diner. His sisters could pay since they seemed to have some plan for him that he wouldn't approve of. He knew the two of them and he'd seen the looks they'd shared.

He and Gertie gathered pretty rocks. Jessie deserved to carry them around in that suitcase she called a purse now. Nothing like the purses Clover coveted and used. Didn't matter anymore. He'd get back in the saddle in more ways than one soon enough. First he'd ride in the charity event. Then he'd be back in the ring. After that, he'd have no problem finding a new woman to squire around.

"Before we go to the market," Lavonda said, "I want to stop by your property."

"Real subtle, sis. What do you and Jessie have planned?" he asked. His niece was perched on his shoulders, wearing his hat, which she had to push at to keep it from covering her face.

"Nothing. I just have an idea for that space but need to see it before I make a decision," Lavonda insisted. Jessie wouldn't look him in the eye.

"You shouldn't fib. That's not right, is it, Gertie?" His niece babbled nonsense in agreement.

He didn't say more but followed his sisters because now he was a little intrigued. He couldn't imagine what they had cooked up at his property. Had they kidnapped Clover and were holding her hostage there? No. Even his overprotective sisters wouldn't do that.

He saw a woman standing in front of the building. It wasn't Clover or anyone else he recognized.

"Surprise," Lavonda said. "This is Jolene. Nearly family. She's Olympia's sister, so by the transitive property she's related, right?" She looked at Jessie, Olympia's sister-in-law. "She's moving to Arizona—and she needs a place to open her business."

"Is that so?" Danny asked with sarcasm. He remembered Jolene from Olympia's wedding, which he'd officiated. She rescued animals or something like that. He couldn't imagine she was opening anything in Angel Crossing, which would soon be swanky Rico Pueblo. Way too soon for his sisters to be setting him up.

Jessie broke into the conversation. "It looks weird, we know, but really we hadn't planned this. Jolene called this morning to tell Lavonda she'd be in town and was looking at rentals. Blame the real-estate people. They suggested your property."

"Uh-huh," Danny said, believing only about half of what Jessie had just said. "Let's go say hello. She's not married, right?"

"No idea," Lavonda said quickly. "It's not a setup."

Danny kept his mouth shut as he put his niece on the ground and took back his hat. Today was as good a day as any to start his new life. Might be the beer and sugar talking, but it was a good idea. "Hello," he said, reaching out his hand. "I'm Danny and I understand you're looking to rent a place?"

"Jolene James," she said, shaking his hand with strength. "Maybe. Depends on what you want to charge me."

"Rent in Angel Crossing is reasonable. What kind of business are you considering?" He and Jolene toured the property as she explained she wanted to open a pet store that also offered homeopathic remedies and rehoming services for pets and ranch animals. It sounded overly ambitious to him, but more power to her if that was what she wanted.

"Thanks again for the tour," Jolene said. "It looks like it could work and the rent is very reasonable."

"I do want to let you know that a developer is coming to town and has plans."

"Heard about that. Rico Pueblo, right? It could work for me. Plus, it will be a while until that all gets done."

"News travels fast," Danny said.

"I heard there's a farmers' market here, too?"

"Yep," Lavonda said. "It'll be going on for another hour or so, if you want to stop by."

"I think I will. Can you give me directions?" Jolene asked.

"Why don't you come with us?" Jessie asked. Then Danny saw her nudge her daughter.

"Duncle, please." Or at least that was what Danny assumed the babble meant.

He stared at his sister. Really low using her little girl to force Danny into going with them. How could they be playing matchmaker? He didn't need their help. He was fine. What he and Clover had been doing was fun, but it wasn't more than skin deep. Any feelings he'd had were about his plans, not about him and Clover. He'd finally convinced himself of that after the beers, the pie and the tour of his building.

He walked down the street with his niece once again on his shoulders and wearing his hat. He heard the women speaking behind him about the possibilities of the property, how to best train horses and why jeans gaped at the waist.

"Duncle," Gertie said almost clearly.

"Yes, squirt?" She tried to lean down, almost falling to give him back his hat. He pushed her back in place and took the moist-around-the-brim hat. Then she started drumming her heels on his chest as she squealed long and loud.

"Gertie," Jessie said. "You stop that noise and kicking your uncle, or we won't go pick out a new lead rope for Molly. They have sparkly ones here."

"Darkles," Gertie said on a breath of love and joy. Danny knew that he'd lost her. He put her on the ground.

Lavonda said to Jessie, "What's that diva pony of yours up to? Is she teaching Gertie to ride, too? Or is she too busy starring on YouTube?" Lavonda turned to Jolene and said, "That pony is more famous than one of those viral video cats."

"Her last video did well," Jessie said of her childhood pony with diva tendencies.

"T'ome," Gertie said, tugging on her mother's hand. "Darkles."

"I better go help," Lavonda said as she hurried off.

"Not very subtle," Danny said to Jolene.

"My sister's about the same. Don't worry. I'm just here for the rental property and to buy salve that Lavonda told me about. She said she uses it on her donkey and it heals up anything."

He and Jolene strolled around the market. She was a good companion on a crappy day. See. He was an adult no matter what his sisters imagined. He was already making plans for the next stage of his life. It wouldn't include Jolene no matter what scheme his sisters had hatched. The woman had her own plan, which politely but firmly did not include a bull-riding cowboy.

"Thanks for telling me about the town. It sounds like the kind of place that might be open to what I want to do," Jolene said as the stands at the market started to close up.

"It's a good town. It'll be changing, though, so it's time for me to move on."

"I can understand. Good luck with SAC. I hope to be around for that. Sounds like a good time."

"It will be. We're just out to have fun. We even have an amateur event planned."

"Maybe I'll see you then," she said, waving as she walked away.

His sisters had said goodbye an hour ago, carrying a pink sequined lead rope for Molly along with a silver-and-pink halter. He was glad they'd already left because he needed to be on his own. He got stopped at least a half a dozen times as he tried to leave the market. He wouldn't miss this, would he? When he was out on the road and riding. It was a lot to feel responsible for an entire town. That had never been his intention. Plus, they didn't need him anymore. Right? They'd chosen Van Camp over him. He tried to convince himself he hadn't been hurt by that because it was all business.

He ignored the next three greetings. They didn't want his vision for a better Angel Crossing, fine. Good to remember that. He should be out of here not long after SAC.

"Hey, Mayor," Bobby Ames yelled out from his booth with stuffed and mounted animals in dioramas. "We need your signature on the agreement with VCW."

"No" shot out of his mouth before he could shut up.

"Don't be a sore loser."

"I'm not a loser. Angel Crossing is," Danny said close enough to Bobby to see the hairs in the stuffed animals. Danny wasn't sure where the words were coming from. "I resign as mayor because I can't agree to a project that will destroy the heart of this town."

"Don't you mean that will break your heart?" Bobby asked.

"Shut it or I'll…shove one of these damned football-playing squirrels where the sun don't shine."

His words echoed around the suddenly quiet market.

"That doesn't sound very mayoral," said Clover's daddy, who'd popped up like a gopher from a hole just behind him. He should be back in New York counting his money, not still hanging around the town he ruined. "But what can anyone expect from a bull rider whose brains have been rattled loose?"

The anger that Danny hadn't known he'd been holding back all day exploded. He turned to Heyer and grabbed him by the collar. "A bull rider who treats Clover with respect and love, unlike her own damned father."

Shit. He dropped his hands and stared at them. What had he just said? He couldn't mean it, could he? That he loved Clover.

Chapter Fourteen

Clover looked around Dead Man's Cottage and sighed. She needed to pack. Her work here was done. She was going back to New York and her new office. How had the place gotten so full of her stuff when she was just renting? There had been trips to the farmers' market, where she'd picked up scarves and table runners from the weavers. Then she'd found out about a tag sale. *Thanks so much, Pepper.* That had added an old-fashioned sewing table, a kitschy lamp and a beautiful pot of Native American origin—although no one was exactly sure from which tribe or what decade. The closet in her bedroom, which had started out with a reasonable number of outfits, had exploded. Her mother had sent care packages of clothing.

Looking at it wouldn't get it packed or thrown away. She would have to jettison a lot of what she'd gathered here…including Danny and all of the memories they'd made. Wow. That was sappy. Maybe she needed to start a greeting-card company.

She was being too hard on herself. Every woman was allowed to revisit an old lover. Not that they'd been much to write home about when they'd been teens. Danny had certainly learned a lot since then, which didn't exactly make Clover feel any better about the situation.

Stop obsessing, she told herself. She was an MBA graduate of Wharton. She knew how to get things done. Yeah, hire someone. That made her laugh because that was one of her mama's sayings, much sassier and more understandable than Danny's mother's.

She might like to hire someone for the grunt work of packing, but she'd still have to decide what to keep and what to pitch. That was the real work. Maybe she should call Pepper and ask her to come over. Then she could give her the clothing and household items that others in Angel Crossing could use. The woman had an encyclopedic knowledge of everyone in town and what they might or might not be lacking. They could make it a girls' night. Did she have any wine and snacks to make it really fun?

Her phone rang. It was probably Pepper. No such luck. It was Mama.

"I understand that Van Camp owns Angel Crossing now," her mama said.

"Hello to you, too."

"This is a business call, darlin'. No time for hello."

"You don't care about Daddy's business, unless it means he can't make the next separation payment. I still don't know how you managed that."

"I care about you, and this plan... Well, I just don't think this is what you signed on for."

"I came up with the current plan," Clover said, frustrated that her mama was still trying to convince her to leave VCW.

"I don't think what your daddy is putting his money behind is your plan."

"Of course it's mine. Daddy sent me to Angel Crossing to fix Knox's mistake. Mama, just tell me what you're dying to say." Clover was so tired of the sniping her parents still indulged in after years of separation.

"You've spent too much time in New York. You know that I like to work up to saying things that aren't going to be heard well by others."

What the— "Mama," Clover said, hoping that her level of frustration was clear in those two syllables.

"If you insist, darlin'. Your father is building Rico Pueblo's gated section on a historic site that will be destroyed." Clover tried to interrupt. "He's working fast so the state doesn't find out. He's also lining up the same legislators and the lawyers to oust every one of the current residents. Then he'll build housing outside of town for a VCW workforce. A modern-day company town."

"I made sure the historic site was worked into the plan, and there's no way we can just kick people out of their houses." But she hadn't seen what her father had presented at that executive meeting, now that she thought about it. What had he shown them then? He'd been slick about telling her his paperwork was elsewhere. Damn.

"Darlin', I don't like to be the one to tell you this, but Knox called me."

"He's the reason I came out here." That and the promise of being CFO.

"Not exactly. He told your daddy no. That's when Heyer called you."

Her heart hurt. Why did she let herself think she was his first choice? Why? She wasn't a little girl anymore. "Daddy lied to me from the beginning, didn't he? I've got to stop him."

"I don't think even you can do that."

"We'll see," Clover said, tears in her eyes. She hung up before she started to cry. She wanted to be a CFO. Her response to a crisis was not tears. It was a new strategy.

Danny had been right, or something like right. Her reason for coming to Angel Crossing might have been all about business, but she didn't want to be in the business of running people out of their houses and destroying their community and its history.

Wait. Maybe her mother had misunderstood or was even using Clover as another means of getting back at her sort-of ex-husband. Clover would call Knox, or at least email him.

She'd been so sure she could do it herself and was getting what she wanted from her father, not just the title but also his respect. Now she couldn't understand why'd she ever wanted that from him.

Still, he was her daddy. First talk with Knox and find out if Mama had the right end of the bull.

"Mama said you'd call me," Knox said when he answered his phone.

"Why didn't you tell me?" Clover decided she should be just as mad at Knox as at her father—if it was all true.

"I assumed you knew. You were the one telling Daddy how you'd fix anything I'd done to ruin the project."

"He told me it was a revitalization of the town. I created Rico Pueblo to provide VCW and the residents with a good deal. Everyone would have come out ahead."

"I find it hard to believe he didn't show you any of this. He was so proud. He was going to show Mama how her down-home folks really were willing to sell their history for the right price."

"Are you telling me this is still all about them and their marriage? This is getting beyond old, and now it could ruin the lives of a whole lot of people. We've got to stop them." Clover was ashamed for the first time in her life. Not that she'd never been embarrassed by her fast-talking, tailored-suit-wearing daddy. He'd never fit into Texas, where Clover had always felt most comfortable.

"This is your fight now. I already fought him and I'm done. I'm happy enough in Hong Kong, and I'll be back in New York in a year or so. I've got plans for my life, too, Clover."

She and her little brother had never been close—too much time spent apart with her in Texas and him in New York. She shouldn't have expected him to defy their father for a second time. After all, she was the big sister. Before she could tell him it was all right, he went on. "You can always run back to Mama and Cowgirl's Blues. I've got VCW and that's it. That's the way it's always been."

"I'm sorry. I don't want to make things harder for you. I'll solve this myself. I'm not going to let Daddy change Angel Crossing. Rico Pueblo is dead."

"I wish you luck, and remember that the board still has to approve anything of this magnitude." Knox hung up. She guessed that was as much help as he was going to give. He was right. She could always crawl back to Mama and beg for a job. Where would Knox go? He'd worked only for VCW. He'd only ever had their father, who'd made sure his heir apparent had a Knickerbocker upbringing with private schools, nannies and a seat on the Van Camp board.

Hold on. Knox had a seat on the board. And Clover knew a number of the other longtime members. She couldn't imagine that they'd be thrilled with what her father had schemed to make happen.

She'd call Lavonda, who'd been in PR. Clover'd bet she could spin this so that Heyer would look bad enough the board would make him pull out of the deal. Since this was about Angel Crossing—Danny's town—Lavonda would help, right?

VISITING LAVONDA HAD been a bust. She said that she wouldn't help Clover unless Danny said it was okay. She blamed Clover, more or less, for the mess the town was about to be in. She couldn't really blame the other woman for her attitude.

What next? Should Clover approach Danny? Did she want to? He'd called her names and treated her like dirt. Time, as they say, to put on her big-girl panties—which made her think *thong*, which made her think *hot nights*, which made her think seeing Danny again was a really, really bad idea.

She didn't usually walk away from a challenge and this was more than a challenge. This was her saving the town that her father's plan—the one that she'd opened the door for—would destroy. Danny had been right. Wouldn't he love hearing those words from her? Yes, he would, but she didn't need to say them in front of the whole of Angel Crossing. She needed to find him alone. She knew how to do that. He might not be a creature of habit, but Maggie May was.

Clover waited quietly at the end of the lot behind the diner where Danny let the dog out in the evening. This was the last trip for the night. It had taken Clover that long to work up her courage, outline what she would say and gird her loins against the pull of Danny. She tried to smile at the last picture. It was up there with her big-girl thong.

Maggie May ran right up to her. Danny hung back, his face devoid of emotion. Fortunately, the dusk-to-dawn light and the full moon made the lot bright enough for Clover to read his face. She leaned down and rubbed the dog's head. "How did she take her last baby moving on?"

"Fine. She'll be ready to adopt as soon as I can find the time and money to have her spayed."

"Let me know how much and I can take care of that."

"Of course you can. I keep forgetting you just finished buying up the town."

"I just want to help."

"We don't need your kind of help." He turned away from her, leading Maggie May away with a signal from his hand. The dog looked over her shoulder, definitely letting Clover know that she didn't approve of Danny's rudeness.

"I have a plan." Clover started after him.

"Where have I heard that before?"

She didn't let his back or his cold tone stop her. "You were right." She held her breath but he didn't turn around and open his arms to her. But she hadn't expected him to. Not really. "Did you hear me?"

"I heard you."

"Aren't you going to say something else?"

"What is there to say?" He turned and Maggie May sat, her soft eyes looking at Clover with doggy pity as she leaned against Danny's leg. "You think admitting you were wrong makes it all better? This isn't about us or anything we did." His chest heaved once, twice, before he went on. "This isn't about winning or losing. This is about a town filled with good people who've been trying to survive. You and your father are going to finally break this place. The mine closing a decade ago didn't do what you and your millions in revital-ization will do. How is this fixable? I didn't fight for Angel Crossing to prove I was right or even to make money. I did it because this place matters. These peo-ple matter."

"I know. That's why I—"

"I'm not going through this argument again. This is old ground. Come on, Maggie May." He started back to his apartment. The dog trotted at his booted heels, looking over her shoulder like she wanted Clo-ver to follow.

"Danny," Clover said, not caring that her voice cracked with desperation. "I've got to make this right and I can. I care about Angel Crossing, too." She paused, trying to find the words that would change his mind. "I spoke with my brother, Knox, and we can fix this. He stepped away because of what Daddy wanted to do. He's with me... Danny, I know you don't be-lieve me and I understand why, but believe this—I don't care if my father fires me. I'm going to make sure that Angel Crossing and its history is protected."

"Whatever," Danny said as he continued up the stairs.

"Why won't you listen to me? Don't you see? I'm

doing this for you." *Wait. What?* Why had she just said that? Her chest tightened in surprise and fear.

"That's low even for you," Danny said, half turning to her. "Saying that you care about me, using what we—"

"That's not why I said that. I mean, I do care about you." She couldn't breathe because she didn't just care about him. She loved him. Her feet wouldn't move and her mouth wouldn't open.

"Yeah. That's what I thought you'd say. Go, Clover. Go back to New York. That's where you belong."

She watched him climb the last few steps. She wanted to shout to him to stop. She couldn't because she didn't understand what her heart had just relayed to her brain. She couldn't really be in love with Danny Leigh. That had been teenage beauty queen Clover Anastasia. Grown-up Ms. Van Camp, MBA, had much different tastes and plans.

Her feet finally moved. She found her car and drove back to Dead Man's Cottage. She'd told Danny she'd make things right and he still didn't believe her. How could he when she didn't believe what she'd just admitted to herself, that she loved him. She plopped down in the sagging armchair. She needed to examine all of this. Did she really love Danny? Was she imagining her feelings because she'd been deprived of his very fine body? No, that was stupid. Even as a shallow teen, she wouldn't have been able to convince herself that sex and love were the same thing. Making love with Danny had been, could be again… *Oh. My. God.* She'd loved him. Always. That was why they'd lost their virginity to each other more than a decade ago. They'd been in love.

Okay. Say she really did love Danny. What difference did it make? He hated her for good reason. She'd helped her father implement a plan that would ruin the town Danny loved.

Was she willing to give up on being CFO? Yes and yes. And not just because she loved a bull-riding cowboy. This decision was about her and what she wanted. What she needed. Her choice to fight VCW and save Angel Crossing was her choice because she had more than a shred of dignity and decency.

She pulled in a deep breath and let the tears stream down her face, the ones she'd been holding back since Danny had told her to go at the market. She ached deep inside and she couldn't hold it in anymore. She held her hand across her mouth so no one could hear her sobs, then gave a wet and hopeless laugh. Who would hear? Who would ever hear her? She was horrible at this relationship thing. She hadn't even known she'd loved Danny. Her first lover, her first real boyfriend, the man she'd measured every other boyfriend against. A sob deep from her soul slipped past her hand.

She wanted to run from the pain. She wanted to curl up in a ball and protect her soft underbelly. She wanted to call her mother and ask her to make it all better. The light of the single lamp blurred as tears couldn't fall fast enough from her eyes. Would this hurt ever stop? It had to because she wouldn't survive it.

Finally, her shirt collar a soggy mess from her tears and her eyes swollen to slits of misery, Clover pulled herself from the chair. After a night's sleep, she'd have a better idea how to go forward. Could she stay in the bed, though? Even though the room had been stripped of everything but the sheets, she and Danny had made love there. Dear Lord and his angels. She'd drive out of town and stay at a hotel. There wouldn't be any memories there. Then tomorrow, she'd hunt down her father and explain what she would do if he didn't amend the plan, pointing out that she'd make sure he didn't get any support from the VCW board. After that, Knox could step in and take care of things. Clover'd call Mama and beg her to give her a job at Cowgirl's Blues. She could let Lavonda know the gated community was gone and all the other parts of the plan that would have ruined the town, and *she* could tell Danny. That would be for the best.

She wiped tears from her eyes again and squinted to make sure that she didn't miss any of the twists on the road out of town. All for the best, she kept repeating, her heart skipping beat after beat as her rental moved farther and farther from Angel Crossing and Danny.

Chapter Fifteen

Since the number of hours Danny had been able to sleep seemed to be in inverse proportion to the number of hours in the night, he'd had a lot of time to think and scheme. He might also have been dodging friends and family who wanted to know exactly what he'd said at the market and what he was going to do about Clover leaving. Nothing and nothing. Especially after going by Dead Man's Cottage and seeing she'd cleared out. Obviously Clover was smarter than him. Their…whatever it had been…had no future. Didn't really matter what he felt, right? It didn't matter that the floor had dropped out of his life, worse than when he'd thought he couldn't ride bulls anymore. That his injury had sidelined him in the crappiest of ways. No great wreck. No spectacular last ride.

The whole idea of going back on the circuit by switching up his riding style wasn't what he wanted either. Right now, it didn't seem like he was getting much of anything he wanted, and that was because all he really wanted was Clover in his bed. In his life. His mama would tell him that if wishes were rubies then the whole world would look rosy. He gave a bark of a laugh, and Maggie May yipped. He still missed Hulk but an email with another photo from the puppy's new family convinced Danny he'd done the right thing. He also thought he might have a place for Maggie May: with his parents, which would be perfect because he'd get to see her. Instead, though, he should be focused on Angel Crossing. He was still the town's mayor. And he had a new tenant, Jolene James. She wanted to get her pet boutique up and running no matter what the town became. He had a lot to do to get the building ready.

It was time to snap out of his funk. He had other jobs to bid on and other life decisions to make. Was life in Angel Crossing or on the back of a bull, whether Clover was with him or not?

Regardless of what he wanted to do for the rest of his life, he'd promised Jolene that he'd get the first floor of the old building ready for her.

"Come on, Maggie May. Time to get some work done. Real work, not just thinking about what I want to do." The dog rushed to the apartment door, giving him a doggy smile of delight. Boy, he wished his life were that simple. Then he'd be a dog and he'd be neutered. Maybe not so fun.

"HEY, DANNY," AJ said as he knocked on the door frame and came into the open space that would become Jolene's new store Pets! Pets! Pets!

"Working here." Danny didn't want to talk with his friend. He didn't want to explain what he'd said at the market and he certainly didn't want to talk about the town. The changes were going to ruin Pepper's ideas for improving the health of the residents with community gardens. Knowing his friend, he probably thought it was Danny's fault and he needed to fix it. AJ was all about making Pepper happy.

"I told those women you were busy and working hard. That argument went as far as a cat in the rain."

"The Back Room Mafia?"

"Who else? I was told to come and tell you to go after Clover."

"Ain't happening." Danny wasn't saying anything more on that subject. "Are you sure you don't want EllaJayne to compete at the rodeo?"

"No way." AJ walked over to Maggie May and gave her a pet. The dog licked his hand. "You found a way to save Pepper's plan last time, so what are you going to do this time? If we don't get Van Camp to move along, none of us will be here. I can't let that happen. Pepper and I are halfway done with our house. Faye has that whole alpaca and llama yarn thing going. We can't move along. We can't do that anywhere else."

"I tried. No one would listen to me."

"So you'll just take your lasso and go home? This is Angel Crossing. This is our home."

"Yours, maybe. I was just here because of Gene, and then I got tricked into being mayor. I think it's time for me to mosey down the road. I guess Van Camp showed me that."

"Really? You're going to let that New Yorker beat you?"

"It wasn't the New Yorker. I could have ignored anything he threw at me. It was the blasted whole town acting like I'd done something wrong."

"They got played. Can you blame them? What Clover—"

Danny couldn't stop his mouth from tightening.

AJ shook his head. "So? You weren't lying at the market when you used the L word. Damn, man, you're one sorry cowboy."

"I'm finally a smart cowboy," Danny argued. "I know when to wrap up my ropes and move to the next ranch."

AJ's expression turned serious as he stepped up to Danny. "If you care...if you love Clover, don't let pride or whatever else get in the way. I know how well that works. You were given a second chance with her. I'd say that was the universe telling you what you should do."

"You've been around Faye too long. Next thing you know, you'll be telling me that I've got a scorpion in my rising sun." Danny moved away from his friend, turning his back on what he was saying, the possibility he was holding out.

"It's Scorpio. And what I'm saying is that you loved Clover when you were sixteen. We all knew it. You had such a sappy expression. Then after you—"

"Enough," Danny snapped. "I know. I know. But I can't fix this with a little cowboy magic. This is the real world and Daddy Van Camp has a bottomless pocket. I'm done fighting the 'man.'"

"You're breaking your promise to Angel Crossing. You said that you'd make this a better place."

"It is a better place and will be even better when Van Camp is done."

"Sure, a bunch of gates and mansions and froufrou dogs. That's going to make this better. What about Anita and Rita? Jim's is all they have."

"It's not my problem."

"Maybe. But do you think you'll feel better ignoring it and not going after Clover?"

"You tell me to not abandon Angel Crossing. Then you tell me to go after Clover. Can't do both of them."

"You're the cowboy who rode Tito V, and you're the only bull rider I know who doesn't walk with a limp. You've got some kind of mojo. Use it now. Prove you're more than a pretty face."

"What if I don't want to fix this?"

"Then you're a liar on top of everything else."

"What do I get out of all of this but a lot more headaches? Just like when I agreed to be mayor… against my wishes."

"Why are you acting like such a little girl? You know you want to be the cowboy in the white hat saving Angel Crossing and getting the lady."

AJ might be just a little right, especially about the girl. He did want Clover. More than want her. She was that piece of his heart that he hadn't even known he'd been missing. He knew he couldn't make her stay, but he also couldn't let her walk away without understanding how he felt about her. Could he do the distance thing like his sister Jessie and her husband, Payson, had done? Hells yes, if it meant that Clover was his. Well, there was his answer. "All right," Danny said. "Help me finish up these shelves and the counter. Then I'll be off to save the day like the Lone Ranger and all before lunch."

"Hot damn," AJ said.

WHAT THE— Clover pulled over as the lights from the police cruiser were followed by blasts from the siren. She might have been speeding. She wasn't sure. She'd left Angel Crossing for the final time this morning, making sure Dead Man's Cottage was cleared of her stuff. She'd just… Well, she may have ruined her entire life. She sat waiting for the officer to tell her how much she owed so she could be on her way. She'd go to Tucson, get a flight to San Antonio and then ask her mother for a job, but not advice. She knew that Mama would probably agree with Knox. Clover wasn't up for another fight.

"Miss Clover," Chief Rudy said. "I need you to step out of the car."

She followed his order, not caring why he was here or what he thought she'd done.

"I need you to come with me," he said.

"Excuse me?" Why was the police chief out on the highway and why did she need to get in his car for a traffic violation?

"In the car. With me."

"Why?"

"I don't think you're in a position to ask that."

A pickup raced past, skidded to a halt and reversed, kicking up a sandstorm of dust. Clover and the chief coughed. But she thought she heard him say, "About time."

Out of the dust, his white hat (nearly white, anyway) tilted a little forward, strode Danny Leigh, looking like himself again with his straight even teeth, tanned skin and blond hair. Tall, powerful and slightly pissed off.

"Clover," he said, touching the brim of his hat. "I need to speak with you."

"I don't need to talk to you," she said. She didn't know that she had enough steel in her spine to have a conversation with him. She feared she'd break down and beg him to take her back. "Chief, just give me my ticket, and I'll be on my way out of here."

"I'm giving you a warning," the fatherly man said. "Don't be too proud to say you're sorry and don't be too scared to take the leap." He walked back to his patrol car. Clover snapped her mouth closed.

"What was that about?" Clover asked Danny—more accused than asked.

"I told the chief—" Danny stopped himself. "Hell's bells. I can't do this alongside the road."

"Do what? It doesn't matter. I'm going to Tucson. I need a flight to San Antonio."

"No."

"Danny, I wish you and Angel Crossing well," Clover said. Then she decided that really she wasn't a coward. "I'm a Van Camp. And I can tell you that VCW will not be turning Angel Crossing into Rico Pueblo."

The surprise on Danny's face was genuine, followed by something she couldn't name.

"My brother and I talked with the board and my father's project has been…defunded, is probably the easiest way to explain it. But what it means is that Angel Crossing will remain Angel Crossing. Knox and I are still working out some other details."

"Hell's to the double bells," Danny said, pulling his hat from his head. "That puts a big ol' pin in my plan."

"Not anymore. You can move forward with what you planned. I explained it to Knox and—"

"Not that plan. My other one."

"You mean the charity ride?" She was trying to fill in the blanks and could see from Danny's face that she wasn't doing a good job.

"Maybe I should have sent you a text. I'm messing this up." A car whizzed by, throwing gravel against them. "Come on. At least sit in my pickup. It's not safe standing here."

She hesitated for a moment, then remembered that she was fearless Clover. The teen beauty queen who'd gone after the best-looking boy on a bull. She went with him, working out how to tell him exactly what she thought of him—and of them together, no matter the consequences.

THANK GOD AND his angels. She might have hesitated but now she was following him to his pickup. He had to tell her soon or he'd never get the words out. He also needed to find out more about what she'd said about her daddy and Rico Pueblo. The morning coffee sloshed uncomfortably in his gut. Maggie May gave a growling bark when Clover slid in.

"It's okay," he told the dog. "She'll be staying." Hell. Why had he said that? Because he had bull crap for brains.

"Sweetie," Clover said, holding out her hand to the dog, who'd poked her snout over the seat. "I'm here to… Well, I already told him about my daddy, and now I've got to say the rest of it."

"No." That had come out louder and a lot angrier than he'd wanted. "What I meant is that I've got something to tell you."

"I think it's ladies first," she said, swallowing hard. Her throat moved and he wanted to kiss the ripples under the soft skin. He wanted to hold her hand and tell her that everything would be all right because… because—

"I love you," he blurted out. Silence filled the cab of the pickup. He saw her wide blue eyes, the blush, the clenched hands. Whatever she had to—

"I wanted to say it first," she finally said.

"What?"

"I love you. I wanted to say it first."

He laughed and Maggie May yipped along. "You love me?" He didn't wait for her to answer. He pulled her across the bench seat to him, locking his lips on hers. Clover. She was his. Her taste was like every good memory he'd ever had or ever would have.

Her hands pushed against him. He instantly lifted his head but didn't let her go. He was never doing that again.

"I had a speech. I want to give my speech," Clover said, although she remained so close her breath spread its warmth over his skin. His hands tightened on her shoulders. He wanted her mouth again. He wanted to drown in the taste of her. "I'll make it fast," she said, holding him off even as her eyes softened. "I realized I loved you because I didn't care about being CFO. I didn't care what Daddy thought of me. All I cared about was making this right for you because Angel Crossing is your place. Your heart."

"Not my heart," he said. Then he leaned in to nuzzle her ear and whisper, "You're my heart, my soul, my reason for getting out of bed every day."

She shivered as his lips found her neck. "Not sure I can live up to that."

"You already have." He pulled her to him again, kissing her hard but with a warmth that was for her alone. No other woman had ever made him hot and mushy at the same time. She was special.

"I love you," she said into his mouth.

He pulled her closer and finally into his lap. He wanted her against him, in the place that had felt like an empty gaping hole. Now with her here, it was completely and permanently filled.

CLOVER FINALLY WIGGLED away from Danny, slowly, reluctantly, after the steering wheel had put a permanent crease in her back. He'd let her go grudgingly and with more kisses. She was as giddy as a girl with her first crush, which was just about right since Danny had been her first. She smiled.

"What?" he asked, adjusting his seat and smoothing his hair. It stood up in whorls and tufts where she'd run her hands through it.

"I was just remembering you were my first and now you'll be my last."

"Damned right," he said proudly. "You're a cougar."

"Two years' age difference doesn't make me a cougar."

"Hey, it's my fantasy. I get to say you're a cougar if I want to."

She would not blush but she couldn't stop the flush of heat that added to the near painful fullness between her thighs. She drew in a deep breath because he could take care of that later...and he would. Right now, they really did need to talk. There was so much that had happened and needed to happen.

"We can discuss your fantasies later." He gave her a knowing smile and she shifted in the seat. Had the cab gotten even hotter?

"Not too much later."

She liked that he was anxious to be with her alone and horizontal. She made herself do return-on-investment calculations in her head to slow her heart and tamp down the heat. They needed to discuss what she and Danny could do to help Angel Crossing. Now that she knew he loved her—insert girlie squee—this part would be easier than she'd imagined. "I told you that my father's project is dead in the water. But VCW still owns or has an option on a number of properties. We don't want to just walk away."

"Good," Danny said fiercely, and Maggie May growled in agreement.

"That means making compromises on both sides." This really was a broad-strokes plan. She and Knox hadn't worked out the details... Maybe she should—

"Remember. I love you." Danny's smile lit up the entire cab. "Dear Lord, I do like saying that."

"I love hearing it, and you'd better love hearing me say it all of the time because you are not going to be able to out 'I love you' me."

She took his hand, marveling again at the callouses, its strength and the tenderness she knew he could show.

"Back to business. With a little work and an infusion of cash, I think we can create a strategy that will use some of what you'd been hoping to do along with some of what my original plan would have done. In other words, we could provide the housing and support to those residents who need it, while creating jobs and economic opportunity. It won't be Rico Pueblo, but we might use parts of that to ramp up the economic—"

He held her face and kissed her hard on the lips. "You make me hot when you talk all MBA." He kissed her deeply then softened his lips as he pulled away. She swayed toward him. His denim-blue eyes darkened to indigo. "How did you make me love you even more?"

"My special talent? If I'd known that when I went for Miss Texas, bet I would have won."

"You would have, but then I would have been arrested for punching every cowboy in the audience. Your sexy MBA talent is only for me."

"ROI," she whispered in his ear. "GDP." He chuckled as his mouth landed on hers and she worked on messing up his hair again.

Chapter Sixteen

Clover tried to wipe the sappy grin off her face. Just not possible. She and Danny had played bull rider and the cowgirl go to the rodeo… Well, she had to giggle at the memory, or she'd end up all hot and bothered again.

"What?" Lavonda asked, sitting beside Clover in the metal stands of the small outdoor arena where Clover had watched Danny practice and now would watch him compete again. Lavonda had told her this was where she'd met her husband, who'd been competing at the Highland games here—a kilted cowboy with a passion for archaeology.

Clover was not telling Danny's sister about anything they'd been doing.

"Yuck," added Jessie, Danny's oldest sister, corralling her daughter between her long legs. "I know that kind of look because you get it, Lavonda. It has to do with—" she looked down at her little girl "—grown-up stuff."

Clover refused to blush because it clashed with her hair. "Look, it's the peewee riders," she said to distract the women.

SAC Bull-Riding Extravaganza, which was still

raising money for the town's new revitalization projects, had everything from three-legged races to bull rides by the top professionals. Best of all, the stadium was full of spectators and every concession stand had a line, including the one run by Pepper's mother, Faye, where she and the ladies from the Back Room Mafia were telling fortunes and giving out horoscopes. They also had a "Take a Selfie with Ralph the Llama" booth, and the line was three deep. Apparently, Ralph had a big Instagram following.

Clover knew she should be nervous for Danny. He would be riding, just for fun—although she'd seen some betting going on between the men, when she'd gone down to wish him luck. He said he was in good shape, having worked on riding left-handed. Of course, she may have distracted him when he'd been working out. What could she say? A big blond cowboy doing push-ups was a thing of beauty. She'd needed to show him her true appreciation.

"Oh, crap," Pepper said from her seat next to Clover. Butch, her "herding" dog, had slipped into the arena, then proceeded to chase the children and the younger llamas who'd been recruited as "wild" bull substitutes. "Butch," Pepper yelled, standing and ready to run into the ring. Then a streak of red and white came hurtling into the fray. It was Maggie May. She'd attached herself to Butch, feeling the need to treat him like one of her pups, while he adored her with the burning love a teen boy had for his first crush. Maggie May nipped at Butch, who stopped what he was doing and lay on his back to show that he was defeated. Pepper laughed. "That silly dog. I'd better go help—"

"Never mind," said Lavonda. "The menfolk are taking care of it."

All four women laughed as Jones in his kilt, Danny in his white cowboy hat, AJ in ripped jeans and Payson in chinos began rounding up the llamas and the scared children. Danny turned and squinted into the stands. *He's looking for me*, Clover thought to herself as she waved. Her stomach dropped at the gorgeous sight of her cowboy. She lifted her matching white hat, with her signature dyed-pink snake-skin band to which a few rhinestones had been added to match one of the purses her mother had started to design with a little bit of input from Clover. She blew Danny a kiss and *wham*. One of the llamas rammed him bull-style then galloped over top of him.

Clover ran down the metal stairs, nearly decking a mom and her kid when they got in her path. She couldn't see the dirt of the arena because so many people had gathered around the railing to watch the kids and now Danny lying hurt on the ground as llamas and dogs raced around.

"Out of my way," Clover said, elbowing people as she'd learned to do at every New York City crosswalk. She got to the dirt and a security guard put out his hand. She growled just like Maggie May and the man shrank back. She sprinted to the circle of men, ignoring the two dogs now calmly rounding up the llamas.

She pushed at the kilted man and finally moved him aside. Danny sat in the dirt, his cheek bruised and his hair matted with…green goop that smelled…worse than manure after a hot day in the sun. Yuck. "Are you okay? Do you have all of your teeth?"

"Teeth?" he asked blankly. "Nope. Didn't lose my cap. Just a little bruised," he said.

AJ added, "And you smell like crap. That's the first time any of the furballs has spit on a human. Feel privileged, Danny."

"Women somewhere probably pay good money to be slathered in llama spit."

"They do not," Clover said. "Let me help you up. Since your *friends* are being as helpful as a tiara on a pig, I'll take you to the showers. This is a college—they've got to have a locker room."

Danny stood on his own and Danny's brother-in-law, the surgeon who hadn't even been examining him—men!—handed him the dented and dirty white hat. She teared up looking at it. Wasn't that just like Danny? All white knight under the dirt and the dings.

He put his arm around her. "Maybe I need help getting into the showers?"

Did he just wiggle his eyebrows? She looked for help from the other men. They had scattered. "You stink," she said, pushing at him. Llama spit was nasty stuff.

"I'm sorry I scared you."

He did it again. Just when she thought he was nothing but a bullheaded cowboy, he'd say something sweet or smart or just so Danny.

"You did scare me. Why did you wave to me instead of watching for the animals? You're a cowboy. You should know better."

"I do know better. It was your rhinestones. They dazzled me."

"So, now it's my fault?"

"Sure is, ma'am. I'm just a cowboy in love and stupid with it." He kissed her before she could say no, and suddenly llama spit smelled a lot like sexy cowboy.

When they broke apart, both of them were breathless. Good. She didn't want to be the only one getting hot and bothered. Whew. He smelled horrible. Amazing what a kiss could make her forget. "Get in the showers now or you'll get kicked out of the competition."

"You, too."

"What?" She raised her hand to her face. Ee-ew. She had a blob of llama spit on her face. "Get it off."

"We will," he said calmly. "The locker rooms are right here. Too bad they're not coed." He gave her another eyebrow wiggle.

"You are one sick puppy." She hurried into the building. She had to get rid of this smelly mess so she could go check on Danny and make sure he wasn't hurt. She knew one thing about cowboys. They were never hurt until they passed out from loss of blood.

"I'm COMING IN," Clover yelled into the men's locker room five minutes later. No answer. That probably meant no one else was there—but it could also mean that Danny had passed out. She walked inside to stop her imagination from going any further. "Danny?" Then she heard the whistling. What was that? It couldn't be. "Barbie Girl"? Before she could shout his name, he belted out the chorus and now she laughed out loud. Her cowboy was a surprise every day, which made her love him even more. Darn him.

"Danny," she shouted as she stepped up to see him washing away in the large open shower area. He jerked around guiltily—as he should. "Practicing for karaoke night at Jim's?"

"You can't be in here."

"Really? I'm here."

"I mean this is the men's locker room."

"I know. But I'm here to check on you. To make sure you don't have a bone sticking out somewhere that you neglected to tell me about."

He gave her a grin that somehow married sexy man with immature teen. "Wow. You might be right." His eyes looked downward, which made her glance the same way. Darn him. They couldn't do anything about that particular problem right now. She was beginning to feel distinctly hot, too.

"Go back to 'Barbie.' I'm out of here."

"Sure you don't want to make sure nothing is broken?" How could he waggle his eyebrows with water running down his face?

"Later."

"But I'm not sure that I can sit a bull like this."

"You're not sitting a bull no matter what."

"I am."

"Are not."

She drew in a breath, refusing to get pulled into a juvenile argument. "Danny, you knocked your head when you fell. You had to. You've got a huge bruise on your face."

"It's a small bruise and I didn't hit my head, just got a tap on my cheek. I organized this whole thing... well, with Lavonda's help and maybe a few others, but I can't not ride. People paid to see 'real' bull riders. I'm one of them."

"You *were* one of them."

"I'll always be a bull rider, just like you'll always be a beauty queen."

"Not the same thing. And I've not been one for a long time."

"To me you'll always be a beauty queen." He started out of the shower and she backed away.

"We'll talk about this when you're dressed. And saying silly things like I'm still a beauty queen will only convince me that you really did hit your head."

He moved faster than a wet, naked man should and pulled her into his arms, nuzzling into the crook of her neck so he could whisper in her ear, just a minor distraction from the big, wet, muscled male smashed all up against her. "I don't need a hit to the head to make me loopy. Seeing you in the stands with those tight white jeans and that hat is all it takes. What can I say? I'm a sucker for a Texas beauty queen." He kissed her neck and she held him and his lips there for a moment.

As she tugged on his hair so she could see his face, she said, "Flattery will not convince me you should jump on the back of a bull."

He moved his hips forward. "What about giving you a bull ride?"

"First, that's a bit of bragging, and, second, we're in a men's locker room. Now stop and listen to me." She stepped away from the temptation of him. Was she as juvenile and hormonal as he because she needed to put distance between them so she could talk to him like the rational, MBA-carrying woman that she was? "Everyone will understand why you can't ride. You've been hurt."

"I know you're trying to protect me."

"Darn right. Since you won't do it for yourself."

"Clover," he said softly. She turned to him again, unable to stop herself. He had a towel around his waist now and an earnest expression on his face. "I need to do this for me, too. You know, I never got a retirement ride."

How could she not have known that? She was supposed to love him. "Why didn't you tell me?"

"I'm telling you now because I just kind of figured it out. I'm good with not being a bull rider. I'm okay with that being my past, but I want to put a bow on it. I want to say goodbye."

"You want to leave on your own terms. I get that." She did. She understood needing to make your own way in the world. That was what she planned to do in Angel Crossing and with Danny. "Get dressed. You've got a bull to tame. Then later I'll ride the bull snake."

He laughed and hugged her. "That's not a thing, and it's about as sexy as granny panties."

"You've never seen *me* in granny panties, then." She kissed him long and hard, knowing once again that her future was here with Danny.

DANNY SETTLED HIMSELF onto the back of Thunder Jr. The bull was new to the ring, and SAC was the kind of ride that Dave the stockman insisted would provide a good show without testing the mettle of the riders too much. Danny thought that his mettle needed to be tested. This competition was his real retirement ride, win or lose, but he'd like to win. He owed it to himself, just like he'd told Clover. To say his final goodbye. He loved bull riding, but it wasn't number one in his life anymore. That was what it had to be for him to do it well. But now number one in his life was Clover, and Angel Crossing, his family, his friends.

"Yo, man, pay attention," AJ said as he thumped Danny on the back. "I thought you'd been practicing."

"I have been. I'm good." This really needed to be his final ride, if he couldn't even keep his head in the game while sitting on pounds of steely bull flesh ready to rid itself of the annoying cowboy on his back.

Dave said from his other side, "This little guy is new. Be nice. I've got big plans for him. Give them a good ride, but nothing fancy. Okay?"

Danny nodded, reached up and settled his slightly dinged-up hat on his head. Give the crowd a show. That was what he'd do. He'd enjoy the ride like he'd done as a teen, when not so much was at stake. Today was about giving the audience what it had come to see and raising money for Angel Crossing. Before he let his brain drift to places it didn't belong, he gave AJ the signal. The chute opened and Thunder Jr. didn't move. Hell's bells. Dave smacked the bull on his beefy haunch. He still didn't move. Frozen. Could a bull get performance anxiety?

"Give 'im a nudge, Danny," AJ counseled. Danny did and the audience yelled, expecting Thunder Jr. to explode out of the chute. But the large black-and-white bull took one dainty step after Danny urged him to move with a gentle nudge from the point of one boot in the bullish armpit. Thunder Jr. turned his head to give Danny a hurt look, like somehow he'd betrayed him.

He tried a tap of his heels, readjusting his grip. The bull stopped dead again, his large head turned so he could look at Danny with one brown eye. What did the animal want? This was a time for them both to shine. Next, the rodeo clowns came out. They looked at the animal warily but approached him, waving their arms. Thunder Jr. bellowed at them but didn't move.

"Okay, folks, it looks like Danny Leigh has already tamed this bull, so we'll be seeing him ride later."

The clowns carefully scooted to the rear of the bull and walked him with Danny on his back out of the arena. As they passed the fence, Danny lifted himself off the bull and waved to the crowd. He watched Thunder Jr. saunter away without a backward look.

What did Danny do now? Ride another bull? Was this the universe telling him that he'd pushed his luck as far as he should? Obviously, he'd been hanging around Faye too much if he thought that. Look at all of the good things he had. Did he really have to win this little bull-riding extravaganza to feel right with his retirement? Clover waved to him, the rhinestones on her headband and those decorating her shirt nearly blinding him in the Arizona sun. What did he need to ride a bull for? His life was going to be filled with more thrills and spills than he could imagine, hooked up to Clover. Time to give other cowboys a chance for glory. He was happy to be Mayor Danny of Angel Crossing and a cowboy for Clover Van Camp. What more could he want? *Babies*. Crap. Where had that thought come from? Thunder Jr. stopped, turned his front quarters and bellowed right at Danny. Dang. He must have hit his head when he and the llamas went two rounds.

"Hurry up," Lavonda said as she sprinted up to Danny after his "ride," then headed around the back to the arena.

Clover stood in front of him now, tugging on his hand. "Come on. We can't miss this. It's going to be the biggest thing in Angel Crossing since Anita got Jim's in her divorce."

He followed the women without argument. This day was supposed to be a good old-fashioned rodeo to raise a little bit of money and the hopes of Angel Crossing. They ended up just to the left of the chutes. AJ stood on top of the gate, decked out in his cowboy best. He must have changed. He'd mess up his clothes if he rode like that.

The announcer's voice boomed out. "We have a little change in the schedule, folks. Instead of AJ Mc-Creary on Widowmaker, we will have a brief performance by AJ on banjo." There was a hushed silence. "Just kidding. That cowboy can't carry a tune in a bucket."

Danny saw AJ's horse Benny come into the arena. His friend jumped on the horse as he galloped past. "What the hell is going on?" he asked Clover, who shushed him.

He looked back to his friend, waiting for whatever was going to happen. His sister looked like she was about ready to explode. Then Jones came sidling up beside her and whispered something in her ear. Lavonda smiled and stared even more intently at AJ and Benny.

The audience stayed silent. Then the horse and rider made a perfect turn and magically AJ unfurled a banner. The rider and horse moved even faster around the ring as the banner whipped behind them. Finally, Danny saw it.

Pepper Bourne, Will You Marry Me? was written in large tie-dyed letters. Danny heard the crowd stirring, and then Pepper was flying down the stairs and into the dirt arena. Benny reared up, Trigger-style, before planting his feet well away from Pepper. AJ jumped off and went down on one knee. He held out the small box that stirred fear in every cowboy's heart. Pepper pushed it aside and landed on AJ, kissing his face and hugging him.

"Guess she said yes. Give them a hand, everyone," the announcer said. AJ and Pepper stood up, still kissing, until the announcer cleared his throat. AJ boosted Pepper onto Benny and led her and the horse out of the arena. He waved to the crowd and Pepper kept her eyes only on him.

Lavonda finally said, "Perfect. I knew he could do it."

"You planned this?" Danny turned to his sister.

"Helped. AJ had the idea. Those two are all about the public displays of affection."

"Don't think I'll do any such thing," Jones said to Lavonda.

"We're already married. You're safe for now. On our fiftieth anniversary, though, I'll be expecting something just as sappy." Lavonda took her Scotsman's hand and led him off.

Danny wasn't surprised that AJ and Pepper would make everything official. It was just that… Wow. He never would have imagined his honky-tonk buddy would go for something like that.

"It was very sweet. I wonder if anyone got a video. It could go viral, put Angel Crossing on the map."

He nodded absently. Why wasn't he thinking that AJ had gone loco? Not because he'd asked Pepper to marry him, but the way he'd asked. It just wasn't *cowboy.*

Clover stepped up and kissed him. He automatically grabbed her around the waist, not caring who saw him kiss her.

"So how are you going to top that?" she whispered against his lips.

Chapter Seventeen

Clover was supposed to be looking at the blueprints Danny had pinned to the wall—instead she was admiring his jean-clad, cowboy-muscled butt.

"You're going to make me blush," he said without turning around.

"Why would you be blushing?"

"Because you're ogling my butt."

"I am not." It wasn't like she was really all that embarrassed for admiring the view. She just didn't want Danny to think he was all of that and a case of Nutella. "There's no way—" Darn it. Clover hadn't noticed the dusty mirror that made up a section of the wall in the old warehouse building's office. "Guess the cowboy who worked here was vain, too."

Danny smiled and said, "Pay attention. This is the first work by Dan-Clover."

"We are not calling the business that. It sounds too much like 'Damn Clover.'"

Danny finally turned around. "If we don't come up with something, Lavonda will. She's already suggested Angelic Architects, which won't work since neither of us is an architect. Or Angel's Fancy, which sounds like a bordello to me."

Clover laughed because he was right and maybe—

"No. Don't even think about it. We are not naming our business that. Why can't it be Leigh Properties?"

"Because I'm not a Leigh. I like my last name just fine and don't see any reason to change it." She saw Danny's eyes go dark and his face tighten into unhappy lines.

"I wish you wouldn't say that."

"Forget about the name of the business or what I want my last name to stay. Let's talk plans." She walked over to the blueprint that laid out exactly what they wanted to do with the warehouse and the surrounding property. It would still be mixed use, but instead of business and residential, it was going to be old and young. Families and singles. She and Danny had plans for it all. They would make it affordable, a neighborhood within a neighborhood. Angel Crossing wasn't one of those places where people didn't know their neighbors, but over time it'd become segregated, mainly by who had how much money. This property would be a place to create a neighborhood that had it all. She was so proud—mainly of Danny. She'd primarily just made sure the numbers added up. He had the vision and creativity. Something she never would have imagined when she'd met the sixteen-year-old bull-riding champion and self-proclaimed (even though he'd been a virgin) ladies' man.

"These are going to look good and be functional, aren't they?"

"They are. I'm glad Knox finally convinced VCW to keep its investment in the business district and sell back the other properties at cost."

"Your daddy is still mad about it."

"Maybe." She shrugged. It hurt that her father had stopped talking to her after she and Knox had convinced the board to abandon his grand scheme. And scheme it had been. Even the board had been a little surprised by the direction her father had wanted to take the company.

Danny hugged her and kissed her temple. She let him, feeling happy and strong, not incompetent. Maybe that was what love was. "I love you," she said because you just couldn't say that often enough.

"That's good because I'm not going to be home tonight. Taking AJ out for his bachelor party. We've got a wild night all laid out. I want you to remember you said that you love me tomorrow morning."

"I've heard about the 'wild' night."

"Karaoke at Jim's can be very competitive, and Rita and Anita told AJ he can only come if he's in costume."

"They did not say that. You and Jones came up with that."

"Maybe. Back to Golden Acres."

"That's not the name of our development."

"Angelic Rest."

"Absolutely not. That sounds like a pet cemetery."

Suddenly Danny looked very serious. Scarily serious. He gently took her face between his hands, keeping his blue gaze locked on hers. "None of this would be happening without you. But that's not what has me puffed up like a rooster with a flock of happy hens." She knew her smile wobbled but his gaze didn't move. "You. Knowing you love me, that you believe in me and what I can do. I'm stunned, amazed every day that you're here. With me. Danny Leigh, big bad bull rider who never went to college and is content to live in a town small enough to make Mayberry look like a city."

"Stop," she said, putting her hands on his. "Who else would I be with? You're the man who knows me and doesn't flinch from the ugly parts—and there are some of those, and I'm not talking about how I'm knock-kneed. I mean that you don't flinch when I get petty and vain. *And* you make me not want to be any of those things. You make me want to be my best." Her smile got wobblier. "Where else would I want to be but in your arms as first lady of the town whose heart is big enough to accept a New York City cowgirl."

Danny's kiss was soft but not tentative. She could feel all of his love in that caress. She never wanted to be anywhere else but in his arms, no matter how clichéd that was.

THIS WOMAN COULD turn him into a puddle of warm pudding with three words and the touch of her lips. He made sure all of his love, laughter and hope was in his gentle kiss. He wanted her to know she was cherished by him not because she slept with him or even because she made her special Texas brand of brownies. It was because of her. All of her curves and all the places she said were flaws. They were spice for him. They gave her shadows, making her highlights even brighter. Dear Lord and his angels, he was sappy. He smiled against her lips. "Glad you can't read my mind."

She moved her mouth to whisper in his ear as her hips moved seductively forward. "Oh, yes, I can."

"Ha. I wasn't thinking about that."

"Somebody was."

"Always said Durango had a mind of his own." He buried his face into the curve of her neck where the special, never-found-in-a-bottle scent of Clover always was the strongest. He wrapped her tightly in his arms, whispering again and again. "I love you."

When he finally finished telling and showing her that he loved her, Danny carefully pulled away, his fast breathing matching hers. "Weren't we discussing Shady Cactus?"

"Lavonda said she'd come up with names for us, and," she added before he could break in, "we'll listen to her for our project because she's done this for very successful Fortune 500 companies."

"But we don't need to be on that list and look what she named her own company—Reese Tours. That's got no pizazz."

"Until everyone meets the little donkey she named the business after."

"I don't know what it is with my sisters and small equines. Jessie's pony Molly is famous around the world because of that video of her at the wedding."

"And for that one where she gives kisses to all of the children at Hope's Ride." Clover smiled at his cranky comments. His sisters still treated him like he was an annoying little brother.

"We'll listen to Lavonda but do what we want. Isn't that what we've been doing since…well, since we met at that Texas rodeo?"

"I guess," Danny said. "We'll discuss the name later. We've got to make decisions about this rehab. The architect gets paid by the change, by the way, so let's keep it simple."

"You mean KISS."

"What?"

"Keep it simple, Sinbad."

"That's not how it goes," he said with a laugh.

"Could be."

"Are you saying the complex should be called Sinbad Acres."

"Now, *that* really doesn't make sense."

"You know what does make sense? You, me and Elvis. Come to Vegas with me and we'll get married now. Today."

"I'm not getting married by Elvis."

"Is that the only reason you're saying no to my proposal?" Clover's bluebonnet gaze went bright with tears and his chest caved in. "Forget I said anything."

"I want to say yes, but...not yet."

He pulled her into his arms because she was worth the wait. She was worth any trials she put him through. "I love you, with or without a ring, and until the cows and kittens come home."

She grabbed his face and pulled it to her, breathing out "I love you" as she devoured his mouth.

OF COURSE, THERE was a pony with flowers and a lacy pillow walking down the aisle toward Pepper and AJ, with AJ's daughter, EllaJayne, leading Molly, the high-stepping Shetland pony. None of that mattered because Clover really thought the star of the show was Danny standing at the end of the aisle with a folder of papers, the vows AJ and Pepper had written. The two hadn't wasted time after the SAC Bull-Riding Extravaganza, which had raised enough to fix up more vacant lots for gardens and start a little nest egg for beautification projects—the council was deciding between new trash cans and old-fashioned streetlights.

Clover was brought back to the wedding by the laughter rippling through the crowd, seated in folding chairs of all types in the recently dedicated Angel Crossing Parking and Multiuse District. Today was its first time as a wedding venue, but it made sense since this was where AJ and Pepper had first met, when his truck had broken down and his daughter had run away to be found by Pepper. Now whenever the two of them were together, their love was obvious to every single person there, including their daughter—Pepper had adopted the young girl with the inky curls and sparkling mahogany eyes.

"Molly—" Jessie's voice drifted over the crowd "—behave or no gummies." More laughter rippled through those seated.

EllaJayne said clearly, "Granny Faye told me we having sleepover so Mommy and Daddy can make a sissie for me."

Molly nodded her head in agreement. Clover couldn't read Danny's face exactly. He looked a little pained—maybe he shouldn't have worn his fancy boots, the ones he'd gotten for going eight seconds with some bull or another.

EllaJayne got Molly moving again and Rita and Anita, on cue, started the wedding-march music, which for this couple was "Baby Elephant Walk," chosen by EllaJayne. Then everyone turned as Pepper started down the aisle in a beautiful gown of blush pink with lace, sequins and pearls. The color made Pepper glow, or maybe that was love, Clover thought, smiling at her own fancy. Her gaze landed again on Danny, who wasn't looking at the bride but instead had his attention glued to her. *Oh, my.*

DANNY HAD OFFICIATED at more weddings than he'd ever imagined he would when he agreed to be mayor, but this one had to top all of the others. All of Angel Crossing had turned out, plus a lot of friends from the rodeo and a contingent of family from all over the country. Even his daddy and mama had shown up. Their RV was parked at Lavonda's. AJ and Pepper had decided that their wedding would be something like a midsummer party. Faye had suggested the date because it was the longest day of the year, and it meant more party fun.

Danny thought that was about right. He took a sip from his longneck beer encased in a coozy that the couple had given out to everyone, which was embossed with the words *Love means never having to say you're sorry but always saying, "Yes, sweetheart." :-)*

He looked for Clover, who'd fit into Angel Crossing like a round peg in a pegboard, something his mama had said this morning. Clover had smiled and not pointed out to his mother that she might have that saying a little…or a lot…wrong. There Clover was with the bride, the pony, EllaJayne and the two dogs, as the photographer tried to snap a shot.

Jessie was there, too, looking hot, annoyed and ready to explode. Danny strolled over and met up with his brothers-in-law, Payson and Jones, and AJ. He knew that Spence—Payson's brother—and his wife, Olympia, and their children were around somewhere, along with Olympia's sister Jolene, who planned to open her shop in Danny's building next month. He already had another tenant lined up because of her. He might need to start an Angel Crossing family tree to keep everything straight.

"Need some help?" he asked Clover.

Jessie answered, "I don't need my baby brother fouling things up."

Payson walked over to his wife, took his daughter from her arms and kissed Jessie. Danny wanted to say "Yuck" like a twelve-year-old. That was his sister, man.

Pepper said, "We're just trying to get one picture that's a reenactment of the wedding procession. I want to make sure I have a good one."

"Molly says more gummies," EllaJayne wheedled.

"You've had enough of those," Pepper said firmly but with no anger. "Can you and she stand just like you did in the aisle?" EllaJayne tugged to get the pony beside her. Molly stamped her little hoof. The pony, who'd been Jessie's as a little girl, was a diva of epic proportions. Somehow they all gave in to her demands. He watched the little pony, and she stared right back at him. He might have been a bull rider but he knew that look.

"EllaJayne," he said as he walked over to Molly, "let me help." His sister Jessie relaxed a tad. She'd seen the look, too. He couldn't imagine that the pony would do anything to the little girl, but the adults and even the dogs might not have been so lucky. A braying started from somewhere over Danny's shoulder and a rumble of laughter and shouts followed. It couldn't be.

"Reese." He heard Jones's Scottish-accented voice above the crowd.

Crap. The miniature burro had more personality

than Molly. Lavonda had insisted that he'd known he was missing something today.

The crowd parted and there was Reese, ears pricked forward before he opened his mouth and let out another hoarse bray. Molly tossed her head and whinnied back.

"Grab the beast," Jones said, still making his way through the crowd.

"I've got Molly," Clover said, taking the pony's rhinestone-studded halter from him, which looked a lot like her hatband. He grabbed Reese's black leather halter. Jones and his sister Lavonda stopped at the edge of the circle. And there was his mama and daddy along with Jolene, Lavonda... Hell's bells. It was everyone.

"Look, they kissing," EllaJayne said as the pony and the little burro touched noses. He'd barely noticed that the animal had reached out because after taking in the circle of friends and family, he'd had eyes only for Clover. Her blue gaze had locked on his. He couldn't hear anything beyond the beat of his own heart.

He wanted the words to come out of his mouth. He wanted to ask... Not that. Clover had made it clear she wasn't ready for that. "Ouch." He looked down and saw Molly's hoof on his shiny boot. She'd just stepped on him.

"Molly," Clover admonished, "that wasn't nice."

The pony lifted her foot and stamped it down again. He heard a number of female voices say the pony's name, and then Reese wrenched his head forward and bumped into Molly. She grinned at him before lashing out with her teeth, causing Reese to buck, kicking out his back legs, just missing Jones, who swore with proficiency.

"I told you, Molly…" His sister Jessie's voice lifted above the others as Danny saw her latch on to the pony's halter. "One wedding a year."

"Reese, my man," Jones said, pulling the burro toward him. "He doesn't need any help."

What was happening? "If a llama shows up, I'm out of here," Danny said.

"My beauties aren't close," Faye said.

"Uh-oh," Lavonda said. "He's got that look, and I don't mean Reese."

"Oh, man, you are so…twirly nailed," AJ amended, looking at his daughter playing with the two dogs who now stared at Danny with some expectation. Maggie May yipped and Butch whined.

"Everyone stop picking on Danny." Clover stepped up to him and took his hand. "Let's go try the Jell-O salad. I haven't had any of that since Mama's Nona Nancy made it."

"No. Wait," he gasped because he couldn't breathe; he couldn't move. This was worse than being thrown from a danged bull. "I…I want… Shi—"

"Don't say that. Little pitchers, big ears," Pepper yelled out.

This was not something he wanted to ask Clover with an audience.

"Danny?" Clover sounded worried.

"I'm fine," he answered with assurance. As sure as he'd been at sixteen and he'd known he had to ask out the eighteen-year-old beauty queen. "Clover Anastasia Van Camp, will you—"

"Don't you dare, Danforth Clayton Leigh," his mama said.

What sort of conspiracy was going on? He just wanted to get the question out. He just wanted to—

"Take this." His mother handed him her engagement ring, the one his daddy had given her and that had been his mother's mother's ring. "You can't ask a woman to marry you without a ring," his mother whispered into his ear with tears in her voice.

He took the ring and looked at Clover. Her eyes were wide, surprised, scared…and filled with love. Molly smacked him in the back with her bony head. He stumbled into Clover. She caught him and the two started to fall, but hands from the crowd around them kept them on their feet.

"I want to kneel," he said to no one and everyone.

"'Nother wedding," EllaJayne squealed.

"Shh," all of the women hissed at her.

He did kneel then, and the dogs came to his side, panting a little as everyone looked at Clover. Beautiful, funny, wonderful Clover. "Clover Anastasia Van Camp, will you—"

"Wait. I'm not—"

"Dear Lord, his angels and Corvairs. I just want to ask you to marry me." A stunned silence, a growl from Maggie May and another knock from Molly.

"Sure. But I'm not changing my name and I get to have as many rhinestones on my dress and hat as I want. And—" Danny grabbed her and the crowd erupted into Wild West shouts.

Clover couldn't catch her breath. What had she just

said? Darn it. That wasn't how you answered a proposal. "I want a do-over."

Danny shook his head. "You heard her. She said 'Sure.'" He laughed, throwing back his head and ending it on a whoop of triumph.

She pulled his head down to her. "Wait."

"No more waiting." He kissed her and another cheer deafened her and shook her heart and soul.

"Danny," she whispered against his lips. "I love you."

"Good to know," he said. "I love you, too. But you will be Mrs. Danforth Leigh."

"As soon as you find a time machine and take us back to 1950."

"Is this our first fight?" Danny asked.

"Not a fight. A discussion."

"You go, son," his daddy said. "Start how you plan to go on."

"Gerald, that's horrible advice," his mama answered. Then everyone else got in on the discussion. Clover pulled Danny away and only Molly noticed them leaving. She gave a horsey smile and wink. Jessie had been right. There was something a little scary about the pony.

"Now, Danny, ask me properly and I'll answer you properly."

"There's no do-overs in proposals."

She didn't want her acceptance to be the word *sure*. "Then I'm proposing to you." She knelt and took his hand. "Danforth Clayton Leigh, will you be my husband, my lover and my best guy?"

"Sure," he said, pulling her to her feet and into his arms.

Dear Lord and his Corvairs, the man could kiss and, better, he could love her like no other.

When he finally gave her a little space for a breath, she said, "I expect this to last for more than eight seconds. I know how you bull riders can be."

"When you're riding the bull, time stands still, you know."

"I might know that but let's test it out again tonight while you show me again how much you love me."

"I'll do that. And I'll convince you that you want me to brand you with my name."

"I'll let you try, but it'll take you more than one night to change my mind."

"Is that a challenge?"

"Challenge or promise—I know that we'll both love it."

* * * * *

*Single mom Molly Griffith and rancher
Chance Lockhart have never gotten along, until Molly's
three-year-old son's Christmas wish unites them!*

*Read on for a sneak preview of
A TEXAS COWBOY'S CHRISTMAS,
book two of Cathy Gillen Thacker's popular miniseries
TEXAS LEGACIES: THE LOCKHARTS.*

"So you're really not going to help me?"

"Convince your son he doesn't want to be a cowboy? And have a ranch like mine? Or get a head start on it by getting his first livestock now?" Chance's provoking grin widened. "No. I will, however, try to talk him into getting a baby calf. Since females are a lot more docile than males."

"Ha-ha."

"I wasn't talking about you," he claimed with choirboy innocence.

Yeah...right. When they were together like this, *everything* was about the two of them.

Molly forced her attention back to her child's fervent wish to be a rancher, just like "Cowboy Chance." Who was, admittedly, the most heroic-looking figure her son had ever met.

"I live in town, remember? I don't have any place to keep a baby calf. And even if it were possible, Braden and I aren't going to be here past the first week of January."

Squinting curiously, he matched his strides to hers.

"How come?"

Trying not to notice how he towered over her, or how much she liked it, Molly fished her keys out of her pocket. "Not that it's any of your business, but we're moving to Dallas."

Chance paused next to her vehicle. "To be closer to Braden's daddy?"

Her heart panged in her chest. If only her little boy had a father who wanted his child in his life. But he didn't, so...

There was no way she was talking to Chance Lockhart about the most humiliating mistake she'd ever made. Or the fact that her ill-conceived liaison had unexpectedly led to the best thing in her life. "No."

"No, that's not why you're moving?"

He came close enough she could smell the soap and sun and man fragrance of his skin.

Awareness shimmered inside her.

He watched her open the car door. "Or no, that's not what you want—to be closer to your ex?"

Heavens, the man was annoying!

Figuring this was the time to go on record with her goals—and hence vanquish his mistaken notions about her once and for all—Molly looked up. "What I want is for my son to grow up with all the advantages I never had." Braden, unlike her, would want for nothing.

Except maybe a daddy in his life.

Don't miss
A TEXAS COWBOY'S CHRISTMAS
by Cathy Gillen Thacker, available November 2016
everywhere Harlequin® Western Romance®
books and ebooks are sold.

www.Harlequin.com

Wrangle Your Friends for the
Ultimate Ranch Girls' Getaway

Win an all-expenses-paid 3-night luxurious stay for you and your 3 guests at
The Resort at Paws Up in Greenough, Montana.

Retail Value $10,000

A TOAST TO FRIENDSHIP,
AN ADVENTURE OF A LIFETIME!

Learn more at
www.Harlequinranchgetaway.com

Sweepstakes ends August 31, 2016

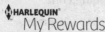

WCHMR